Blood and Steel: Legends of La Gaul
Volume 1

Blood and Steel: Legends of La Gaul Volume 1

Steven Shrewsbury

SEVENTH STAR PRESS

Cover art: Matthew Perry
Cover art in this book copyright © 2013 Matthew Perry & Seventh Star
Press, LLC.

Published by Seventh Star Press, LLC.

ISBN Number: 9781937929282

Seventh Star Press
www.seventhstarpress.com
info@seventhstarpress.com

Publisher's Note:
Blood and Steel: Legends of La Gaul, Volume 1 is a work of fiction. All
names, characters, and places are the product of the author's imagination,
used in fictitious manner. Any resemblances to actual persons, places,
locales, events, etc. are purely coincidental.

Printed in the United States of America

First Edition

Acknowledgements

Thanks to Stephen Zimmer, Jessica Lay, Brady Allen, B.J. McPherson, Chris & Angie Fulbright, Mark Boatman, Jim Mcleod, Ron Kelly, Cheryl Lynne Staley, Peter Welmerink, Bob Freeman, Rhonda Wilson & Craig, Matt Perry, James Tuck, Alicia Justice, Eric S. Brown, Donnise, Noigeoverlord, Michael West, Cherry Wanders, Lisa Mannetti, Alex Adams, Rhonda Harris, Walt Hicks, Angela Bodine, Elizabeth Donald, Andrew Leonard, Val, Gina Ranalli, Ty Schwamburger, Mandi Lynch, DezM, Nikki Howard, Sharon Moore White, Maurice Broaddus, Mari Adkins, Dean Harrison & the Shrewsburys that like my work...Mark Sr, Jr, and Amy.

Thanks always to my family, Stacey, John and Aaron.

-Shrews

Dedication:

To Jessica Lay for her support and being the best thing to come of of Australia since FOSTERS and Olivia Newton-John.

The Tales:

Day of Iniquity

Day of Iniquity

Once Gorias saw that the scribe Jessica sat astride her mount, a beautiful roan several hands shorter than Traveler, he reined his horse about and started trotting for the edge of town. Segesta, a quiet village composed of many brick buildings in its truly clean, metropolitan center, degenerated quickly in the outer reaches, as the streets turned rougher and the homes became made of logs.

"One would think the external limits of a village might be where the new houses start," Gorias related, casting a final glance over his shoulder. "It seems they build in the middle, new atop torn down older places."

Jessica gripped her reins and looked back as well, for a moment. "Why is that, do you think?"

"Perhaps familiarity. Maybe folks don't wanna leave a spot. Maybe just bein' lazy. Who knows?"

"Do you ever dream of the place of your birth?"

Eyes ahead, Gorias' voice held no emotion when he replied,

"No. My boyhood home, maybe a little, but not where I was born."

"Do you miss family and friends?"

"My family back there, where I grew up, are all dead. And what friends I have are scattered."

"Both of your parents are dead?"

Gorias shot her a sour look. "This is gonna be a great time hangin' out with you. Traveling alone provides a kinda silence rough diamonds can't buy."

"I'd love to hear about your parents." Jessica produced a tiny scroll, spread it across a stone tablet balanced on her saddle horn, and then produced a quill from her robe.

"Ya write with that?"

"Certainly. It scribes on the parchment, and I rub it in later with filler."

"Amazin' I say," Gorias deadpanned.

"Was your father a great warrior?"

"Yeah, but he was a chief of our folks in that region of Thule." He gazed off into the rolling countryside and distant trees as he recalled. "We seldom fought unless for a good reason, but every so often, such an event popped up. That guy, he'd travel half a world away to get what he wanted. Took most of the village with him on such treks. He got pissed, he stomped on the reason." Gorias eyed her and asked, "You all right? Ya look like ya got lost all of a sudden."

Jessica turned her face from him, and her gaze wandered in

the sparse, open grasslands before them. "You're giving me hints, not tangible tales."

"The tangible tales of Gorias La Gaul," he chuckled. "I wouldn't pay to hear that even if half drunk. All right, once we get bedded down, ya can use one of them eyes of the dragon, and I'll show you a story about my father and mother."

Jessica looked to him again. "Is it a romance?"

"There's some love to it," Gorias affirmed, eyebrows raised in recollection. "Haven't thought about them in a while."

Jessica smiled wide, then tried to repress it, taking on a studious look. "You will place the eye to your head and pass on that vision to me?"

"Sure. Glad to see you can't contain your excitement. Lemme warn ya, sister, be ready. My visions, and the stuff folks told me about that forms most of the story, ain't pretty."

"The eyes pick up real events seen by those there, or their blood kin in spirit."

"That's the theory about those Eyes of the Dragon anyway."

"You sound doubtful."

Gorias sighed as they journeyed on over a great crest and headed down into a valley. "In every Eye of a Dragon is a negligible flicker of dragon-fire, a part of the soul of all dragons. They desire a window into the life of a person. They got to see plenty of me, so I really don't fret over myself."

"But you do me?"

"Someone has gotta."

Her dainty hand on her chest for a moment, she winked. "I'm touched."

"I'd feel pretty bad if ya got screwy in the head over the things I could show ya and your spirit is tainted by the dragon-fire."

"Nonsense." Her forehead furrowed and she took on a somber expression. "The goddess Ishtar will preserve me."

Gorias' smirk faded. "Good luck."

***

"This area is pretty harmless," Gorias assured her, as Jessica spread out her bedroll near a small campfire in the darkness.

"In reading up on this area, it seemed reasonably devoid of beastie stories."

Gorias stopped for a moment as he removed Traveler's saddle. "Beasties?" he said quietly, and then stowed the saddle. "Yeah, the further inland we get, the worse that is, but we're safe for now. The night is undamaging for now."

Jessica's face lightened up, made almost angelic in the glow of the fireplace as she pulled the Eyes of the Dragon from between her breasts. "What have I to fear? I'm riding with Gorias La Gaul!"

He turned and wondered, "Ya been nippin' at the wine flask already?"

Day of Iniquity

She wore a hurt expression, bottom lip pouting. "I had some Brandywine, but not enough to obscure any coming vision."

He pondered her words and how she only feared a night monster, or a snake maybe, but not the amorous advances of one of the world's greatest lovers. Such was life...

"Well, get comfy and we'll try this out," Gorias told her, as he saw she already had a cross-legged, fitted position with a blanket about her legs.

She was all ready to get his vision. He thought it was lucky for the gal that he was a gentleman, as while in visions folks could easily be taken advantage of. They were entranced for a long time, watching. He shook his head as if to banish the idea of attacking the young lass during the coming experience.

He took the tiny bag of Dragon jewels, shook one out, and frowned at it in the palm of his hand. He then sat before her, but not in the same position.

"What?" she wondered as he groaned, pulling his cloak off and dropping to his buttocks, aimed toward the fire.

"I ain't as nimble as I once was. You live 700 years and try that sitting style ya got working."

Jessica's eyes widened as he picked a jewel, her anticipation high.

Gorias placed it to his forehead, closed his eyes, and then yanked it away. "Here. Go crazy."

She clicked her tongue in her mouth and grinned. "That

easy?"

"Ya need to lay off the Brandywine, missy."

She rocked her hips, swept back her hair, and placed the jewel to her head.

And the rest was history.

***

"You throw down the body of an olden woman in front of the Son of God himself, and expect information?" the deep voice wondered, before stopping to chuckle. "You truly are from the lands of the north near Thule, Chief Ambiorix. Only one from there would have the stones to do such a thing."

Steely fingers held the writhing body of the woman on the slab. The weathered digits attached firm to the muscled arms of an enormous man. Beneath his heavy mustache, his lips curled back and he grunted, "It's you who sets the price of accurate tidings, Neurath. Besides, what makes you so special? There are many sons of the gods running across this planet."

The flickering firelight in the cavern only showed the massive outline of the giant Son of God as he leaned forward. From the shadows came the sound of nostrils flaring and the wet scrape of steel on stone.

Though Ambiorix stood very tall, the figure nearby dwarfed

him. The air soon gasped as a heavy blade passed through it. Ambiorix never flinched as the Nephilum Neurath dropped the axe head the size of a man's chest on the stone slab.

The naked woman wheezed and then let out an earsplitting cry, before her sobs exploded into insane squeals. Neurath clumsily dropped the axe beside the block. He reached down, picked up the skinny leg freed up from the body, and put the bloody edge to his huge mouth.

"Good enough?" Ambiorix asked, still holding the woman down solid.

Neurath sighed. "It will do for starters." The giant then seized the tiny figure on the stone, careful not to drop the leg, and Ambiorix released her. The behemoth turned and hanged her on metal hooks screwed into the stone wall. As the hooks pierced through her back and protruded under her collarbones, Neurath yawned, "So, Ingaevone tribesman, what is it you require of me?"

"What no one else can give," Ambiorix replied, a hand on the grip of a short-sword sheathed at his waist. "I need to know where the cult of Ensibzianna hides. It's said the malevolent son, Alagar, leads these folk at the moment."

Neurath sat back on a cushioned outcropping in the cave, still chewing his food, and soon said through crimson teeth, "You come to a Nephilum for such a boon? You have stones in those russet trousers, I will grant you that, Ingaevone." Swallowing, he gestured with the leg and muttered, "Alagar, curse me running, that damnable imbecile."

"I know the charge of one who thinks he's descended of the gods," Ambiorix stated and motioned to the cave entrance. Two husky men, nearly copies of Ambiorix in large build and hirsute body, carried in a struggling figure, but this time it was an old man. They stripped him of his scarlet cote-hardie, then his gypon, and again Ambiorix held his offering down on the granite wedge.

Neurath arched an already serrated mono-brow. "You came prepared. So the primitives from beyond the Zenghaus Mountains are learning, eh?"

"I'd never travel this close to Shynar unless it was vital to me or my kindred," Ambiorix said as he maintained his pinning clutch on the oldster.

With a single nod, Neurath scooped up his axe and reared back. The old woman hanging behind him screeched and passed out at last. The axe fell, and this time the giant extracted a left forearm from the stone block. Sampling this meat and wearing a more appreciative look, Neurath declared, "Very good, Ingaevone. This mage is from afar." Neurath then arose and hung the man on a set of hooks near to the old woman. The tongue of the aged man screamed curses unto the Ingaevone, their mothers and the offspring of fallen angels.

Ambiorix waited patiently, never speaking.

Neurath noted Ambiorix's patience. The again reclining giant gnawed on raw tissue. "I admire you, primitive human. You hold your tongue." He wiped his ruddy-skinned forearm over a bloody maw and asked, "You knew the price was blood and provender?"

"As is the cost with anything," Ambiorix replied with a calm voice. "All matters come down to blood."

Gulping with a stiff grunt, Neurath sucked on the forearm and wore a reflective expression. "Ensibzianna, aye? A cult indeed worships my half brother Alagar from the heavens. His ego is overloading his ass, truth be told." He fanned himself with the bone, and licked marrow from his upper lip. "I know where he awaits oblations from his foolish admirers."

Since the pause was so long, Ambiorix sighed and turned to his men. They exited the cave and returned with another screaming contribution. Again, this woman was older, but not as ancient as the first one Ambiorix lay down before Neurath.

Neurath's hawkish nose twitched. "You keep the fatter ones for later? You are wise," he snorted, watching the men place her under Ambiorix's hold.

This woman did not cry, but cursed Ambiorix and Neurath. "I invoke the names of Asmodeous and Azathoth to burn out your eyes!" she yelled with enormous malediction. "May Tiphereth mate with your mother! May Belial pass water in the face of your sister and all of her children fall from her belly before it is time!"

Neurath belched a bored groan as he picked up the axe. "Mouthy one, no?"

Ambiorix held her with great difficulty as she made signals

with her fingers, blaspheming heavily. Frowning, Ambiorix said, "I'll throw in a few more if you cut off her head."

With a slight snigger, Neurath chopped and she yelped. He took her left foot off and promptly placed the woman on the wall. Though wailing in agony, she still uttered profanity and curses at them.

The old man next to her had gone unconscious from loss of blood now painting the wall. The giant eyed her, and then Ambiorix. "Maybe you are correct." He then picked up the foot and started to pick at his teeth with the appendage's little toe. "This cult is located in the ruins of Larak at the edge of the desert of Dundayin. This is most certainly true."

Ambiorix nodded, and started to turn away.

"Tell me," Neurath mused, teeth grinding on the cold toes amid the ear-piercing curses of the woman. "Amuse me, Ingaevone. Why does the cult of Ensibzianna enrage you enough to bring sacrifice unto a Son of God that is not of your faith? Why travel all this way from home in Thule?"

"My god is Wodan," Ambiorix responded with assurance. "He gives strength the moment one is planted in your mother's belly and watches us to see if we'll stray from the good course. If I were not smart enough to find my lost blood amongst the cult, Wodan would not show his favor to me."

Neurath nodded, as if lost in thought. He then supposed, "And yet you had no trepidation of bringing these ones in for me?

Day of Iniquity

You fear not their powers? They are all necromancers and witches, as it were, every last one."

Ambiorix shrugged. "Why should I be afraid? I don't believe in their gods."

The cackling laughter of Neurath echoed out of the cavern as Ambiorix exited.

Just outside the cave, the acolytes of Neurath frowned at the savages. The three women were tall, quite fleshy, and dressed in green samite robes. The youngest one stepped forward, her black tresses shaking, and said to Ambiorix, "You fancy yourselves real men? You do not know what it is to be a true man."

Ambiorix didn't reply, but one of his men, a fireplug-shaped warrior called Garretson, cursed the woman and told her, "You fuckin' have courage because you can fuckin' take in a giant? Wodan craps fuckin' knives on you."

They climbed on their horses, but the woman persisted, wishing blight on Ambiorix. Looking down, Ambiorix retorted, "What kind of woman lays down with what is not human?"

She snapped back, "What kind of man brings in old ladies to sacrifice for his desires?"

"One in love?" Ambiorix shrugged. "They were just witches. They said they could tell me where my true love was located." He then smiled wolfishly. "They lied. Take care that I find my love at Larak, or we shall be back."

The other plump acolyte put her arm around the cursing girl

and said to Ambiorix, "She's young."

Garretson pulled on his face wrap to ward off the trail dust and muttered, "She may not get much fuckin' older."

The young woman said, "To give up lives for meat, just for your love, that is barbaric!"

Ambiorix and his kindred laughed. "We are barbarians," he informed her as they left.

***

A grizzled man, ancient of years, opened the door to his home. The small abode, made of mud bricks, was the only structure aside from a grain storage bin at the oasis. Several palm trees and a long pool of bubbling water made the oasis unique on the edge of the vast desert of Dundayin. Wobbling, using a withered branch for support, the crone faced the mounted barbarian horde alone.

"Good day, men," the old one said, shielding his eyes to the sun. The watcher then saw several women dismount from amongst the great force. Not much smaller than the men, these sturdy-built females carried sheathed swords too. He lost count of how many walked in the pack.

The host of hairy men climbed off their horses and led them to the water. There were so many of the barbarians that they refreshed their horses and themselves in shifts.

Day of Iniquity

From out of these strangers emerged two blue-eyed men. Removing the dark cloth from their faces, they nodded at the watcher and shook off the dust.

"I am Ambiorix and this is Garretson. We shall use your water."

Looking back the way they came, the watcher said, "Far from home, I see."

Ambiorix went to the bubbling spring and buried his face in the water. Emerging with a wild gleam in his eye, hair whipped over his head, he looked at the water and then directed his eyes south of the oasis. "Larak is not far from here. I can see the ruins in the distance."

The watcher coughed in agreement and then sat in a wooden chair made of sanded-down palm tree trunks. "Not much there, young man."

Never taking his eyes from the distant site, Ambiorix murmured, "All that matters is there, oldster." He then gestured to his men. They unloaded a few long rolls of cloth and lay them at the door of the watcher. "There's dried meat and nuts in there. We remember who honors us."

"I thank you for that and my life."

Ambiorix's eyes still ignored him, but his mouth replied, "No use killing an aged watchman is there?"

"I suppose not."

"Previous owners of the food have no more use for it. Call it a gift from Wodan."

The watcher faced back to the North. "Wodan? My, you are far from home. By your fair hair and blue eyes, I'd guess you were of the tribes far beyond the Caucaus Mountains nearest here."

"You would guess correctly."

The old man fell silent. He took a few breaths and then looked toward Larak.

Ambiorix waved for the women to refill the skins of water, and at last faced the watcher. "And you wonder why we are here, from a world away, so far south?"

Shrugging, the watchman said, "I'd deduce it has to do with the faction of Ensibzianna in Larak. They absorb many followers and hold up in the ruins. There certainly isn't anything to rob or rape in the remains of Larak."

Ambiorix's huge hands curled into fists. "That's not why I ... we are here." He bent over and leered at the watcher. "Why are you out here at the edge of the desert?"

"My father before me lived and tended this oasis. It's my life. This is where I live and belong. I do as I was taught. Surely, even you folk of the north know to honor your father and his wishes."

"We know of blood, old man," Ambiorix nodded, and walked to his horse. "My niece here is twice the fighter most men are, and worth dying for."

The watcher eyed the stout, blonde girl, barely covered in buckskin clothes and cloaks to keep off the sand. "Take care.

There's a gang of fighters in Larak."

Ambiorix smiled. "That's all right. I brought my own."

With a snicker, the watcher wished, "Be of fine fortune then, even if you meet your death. If you seek after your kin, I hope you find them."

"I will," Ambiorix promised. "If they send my ass back to Thule, they won't send it back alive. The fools in Larak plan a sacrifice tomorrow, a grand hecatomb of children and infants. I know through their by-laws and their slavery to the shifts in the lights of the sky. If anything, these religious dolts are dogmatic and prisoners to their rules. We'll take them all to Hell before any of my kin falls."

"God be with you," the watcher wished him.

"God loves men like me," Ambiorix said, half jovial.

"Why is that?"

Ambiorix shrugged. "He just does."

As the barbarian leader walked away, the other blonde man Garretson looked at the watcher and proclaimed, "God has balls. So does Ambiorix. God respects that."

***

Stopping a fair distance from the ruins of Larak, Ambiorix surveyed the scene. He saw heavy-set men and boys, sorry excuses for guards or pickets, scurrying to tell that a massive force stood at the doorway to the despoiled city. That didn't concern Ambiorix at all. "They need to keep what I want alive," he muttered to no one. "Don't they, now, princess?"

The city of Larak was once a great spectacle, Ambiorix heard tell, but destruction fell on it long before he drew a breath. Previously, his warrior grandfather, Gorian, told him a raging sea once covered the desert of Dundayin. Off to their left, an endless wasteland hemmed in a more fertile ground around Larak; fertile, as to say weeds and some plants grew there.

One of the warriors said to Ambiorix, "Looks as if that land over yonder is the piss bucket of the gods!"

After the laughter subsided, Ambiorix nodded toward the ruins ahead. "My grandfather told me around the fire that Larak was destroyed and he didn't lie. But what sort of creatures could have done that?"

While rows of obelisks remained, several blocks of these phallic stones lay knocked every which way, as if a child destroyed a playground sand sculpture. Numerous high stonewalls slumped, some broken and jagged, whereas others still formed corners. The ceilings of many of the buildings, which Ambiorix guessed as temples, had caved in, spilling light and sand through the breeches. Grim, chaotic visions swam in the primitive skull of the foreigner to the desert. Ambiorix's heart started to beat faster, but he never would have admitted to such a fact. It was as if the structures toppled in a pattern, he thought.

"What vanity," Ambiorix declared, pondering the configurations not overthrown by human hands. "To build up marble houses for their gods to live in, huh, looks like one of them grew angry enough to knock down the habitations."

"Shall we send the new squatters to their fuckin' gods?" Garretson asked, causing a cheer to arise from the multitude.

With serenity in his manner, Ambiorix gripped the handle of a sword on his back. "Yes."

Whichever riders rode two at a time let their spare dismount. As these lines of footmen assembled behind the procession of horsemen, those inhabiting the ruins of Larak scuttled like disturbed rats. Unorganized and half dressed, the residents created unity only in their communal fear; at the shout of the Northern ruffians, heralding their berserk charge.

Shouting with insane vehemence, the invading folk moved en masse toward the broken granite carcass of Larak. Ambiorix felt his blood leap in his veins as the thunder in his ears became drowned out by the cacophony of hooves.

A few dozen valiant souls actually stepped forward to fight. This force of cultists swiftly retreated when they realized the size of the tide of livid humanity bearing down on them.

Swinging long swords, bludgeons, and stabbing spears, the multitude rode into the crumbling streets, slaying whomever they encountered. Ambiorix lead them in first, removing the skullcap of a bald-headed man. The man swung a curved footman's axe at him and missed badly. After one swipe from Ambiorix, a slop of brains painted the nearest fallen obelisk. The ancient mosaic of creatures, of a kind half man and half squid, was further obscured by the gray gruel.

No organized resistance flowed from the cult of Ensibzianna. Since the attack lacked great order, they made the melee additionally turbulent. Most of the savage host leapt from their mounts, dragging downward running members of the religious assemblage. Punching, stabbing and slashing, Ambiorix's people made rapid work of anyone unlucky enough to be caught.

Ambiorix and Garretson met, gathering their troops behind their backs. In front of them stood one of the more complete edifices, hardly cracked by whatever destroyed the city. From this structure poured an armed, fighting force, lean men all in thin chain mail, brandishing shields, axes, and short scimitars. Prepared for their deaths, Ambiorix's tribe screamed for *Wodan* and charged.

Blood spattered the ancient pillars anew, and the dust became muddy in the spilled ichor. Ambiorix looked down at a fallen Ensibzianna cultist. The mouth stretched open too far, crimson sparkling as it ran out fast like vomit.

Helmets flew and heads rolled free from them as Ambiorix's warriors forced their way forward. Links of chain mail bent or shattered under the strength of their strong blows.

A press of fresh bodies forced Ambiorix's fighters back to

a huge block of stone. While three held him in place, one short-haired man grinned and stepped away from the throng. He held up a flail and spun the metal-spiked head around in victory. He gloated too long before delivering the deathblow, for this gave Garretson time to make a diagonal slash and remove the head from the short-haired cultist, nearly taking off his shoulder as well.

Ambiorix pushed off one of the cultists, and this man landed on the end of Garretson's sword. Only impaled through the kidney, the man howled and slipped off the blade, as Garretson cursed. Soon, his left hand swung around, wielding a war hammer. Though the cultist's head did not explode, it did give a loud, wet popping sound, as the body under it plummeted.

Swiftly dispensing with the two left to him via his dagger and sword, Ambiorix nodded to Garretson, and they moved closer to the center of Larak.

Through the massive slaughter, the tribesman ran amok and prevailed. Shoulder to shoulder, they advanced towards the main shelter of the cult of Ensibzianna.

Suddenly, a huge shape stumbled out of a break in the wall. The invaders froze for a moment, but their tension soon passed. Alagar himself entered the fray. However, this giant, twice as tall as even the hulking Ambiorix, was no fiend incarnate. His muscle tone had gone, and his elongated limbs slacked at the biceps. His stomach hung low over the green silken kilt that covered his nakedness.

"Fuck, but he's seen better days," Garretson remarked, holding back a smile.

Alagar staggered, trying to hold up his huge mace to fight.

Ambiorix said, "He was once a lover of great capacity."

Garretson affirmed, "Butcher me to fuckin' Hell if I end up as such."

"Agreed," Ambiorix guaranteed him, and waved an arm at the youths in the tribe.

These boys, barely in their man-making stage, were along on the trip to complete that particular journey. They launched spears at the immense Alagar. Many of the lances broke, stubbled off on Alagar's thick skin, but a few of them held in his belly.

This distraction was all the tribe needed to thrust ahead. Despite the fact that Alagar swung down, crushing the spine of one attacker, the folk swarmed his legs, chopping with great battle-axes, taking his toes and ankles out with ease.

Alagar fell to his knees and swiped his mighty arms, shoving several off him. Ambiorix and Garretson attacked as one, both swinging their swords down at the top of his shoulders.

Ambiorix's overhand swing removed the left arm of Alagar. Garretson's blade swung into the joint of the right shoulder. The giant lowered his brow and thumped Garretson to the dirt. His head swayed to Ambiorix, and with a clumsy impact caused the leader to drop his sword.

Frantic, needing a weapon, Ambiorix performed as all

barbarians do, and fought with what was at hand. He grabbed the wrist of the giant's dismembered arm and shouted a wordless war-cry.

Swinging the limb up, he slammed the bloody stump of the arm into Alagar's jaw. As if he were stabbed, the Nephilum grabbed his mouth, his injured right arm flailing, and blood spurted out.

It was an orange fluid. Ambiorix assumed the giant bit his tongue off from the blow. In moments, Alagar felt the points of a dozen spears in his chest and belly. He slumped back abruptly, and breathed his last.

"At least he fuckin' came out and fought," Garretson commented, sucking air, winded by the struggle.

"He had courage, perhaps as much as any cornered beast, aye?" said Ambiorix, as he turned and saw further members of the cult stream out of the pillar-lined streets. Screwing up their audacity, they meant to retaliate.

Rushing forward, the counter-offensive had some teeth to it, at least until they beheld their dead Lord Alagar. At the spectacle of his bloated corpse full of spears, they shrieked and fled.

"The day is fuckin' ours!" Garretson rejoiced, and many jumped in the air.

Ambiorix looked into the main shelter. "Almost."

Drawing near to Ambiorix, Garretson said in a low voice, "Do you think Neurath warned Alagar that we were coming?"

Peering into the lopsided stone structure, Ambiorix shook his head from side to side. "No. They were ill-prepared for a strong assault. Besides, how could Neurath have done that?"

Garretson thought for a second and answered, "Perhaps a power of the fuckin' mind? They have unearthly parents."

Ambiorix gave him a distasteful glance, and motioned for him to follow along, heading on inside. "I doubt that. Besides, the Nephilum all hate each other."

"Why is that?"

"Imagine a family where all of the children think they are god."

Grunting a little, Garretson surveyed the interior of the barren building. "I see. Still, we killed his brother."

"Neurath will not care," Ambiorix promised as he walked, unarmed, towards the front of the building. "One less sibling to worry about. Neurath would applaud me if I brought Alagar's head to him."

"Will you?"

Ambiorix glanced at him and smirked. "No."

At the echo of their voices, a few people scrambled from behind a crumpled tapestry. These few older men didn't make it out alive, running into a line of thickset savages.

Ambiorix and Garretson never concerned themselves with them. The fallen tapestry revealed a vulgar, decaying stone altar. Once, this small platform was an oversized pair of breasts divided by a phallic symbol.

Day of Iniquity

An unstable world, or whatever trashed Larak, had ruptured the floor in places, thus making the altar uneven and pinch together, crushing the penis between the breasts. This amused the chief, but when Ambiorix walked behind the slab, his smile faded.

"Come on out, dog," Ambiorix snapped, his mouth forming into a snarl.

The figures popped up so quickly that Garretson stepped back and held up his sword. One person was a man of great age. His eyes flared with vitality as his arm easily subdued the woman under his grip. Arm around her neck, his other hand held a curved blade.

The flaring eyes of the man danced as he promised, "Come closer and she dies, dirty pig!"

The woman was much taller than the elderly man. Her ginger-colored hair hung disheveled about a grimy face. She wore a single-pieced cloak, but this simple cover couldn't hide her advanced state of pregnancy. The look in her eyes was one of terror at the sight of the warriors.

Ambiorix scowled at them, and his gaze focused on her. Eyes dancing over her appearance, he reached out an arm to Garretson and took the short sword.

The older man shouted with vigor, "Stop, or I will sever the cow's throat! I will do it as sure as you live. I don't care if she's from the royal house of Transalpina. I am a priest of Alagar, and ready to die, so back away or I shall cut her from ear to ear."

The blade of the short sword bounced off Ambiorix's thigh. He said coldly, "Do as you must."

Confusion reigned in the eyes of the priest as his gaze went from Ambiorix to Garretson. From out of the tresses, the woman also registered bewilderment. Tears started to flow from her bulging eyes.

"I said," the old cleric repeated. "I will kill her!"

"Kill her then," Ambiorix told him as he stepped forward.

The priest and woman bumped into the stone slab as Ambiorix's left hand reached out. However, he never grabbed at the old man nor the woman's arm to pull her free. Instead, he placed his hand lower, on the flat in her middle, below her breasts, above her stomach.

With an almost elegant thrust, Ambiorix sliced a crescent wound around the belly of the struggling woman. The priest released her, his voice caught in his throat, and she sprawled on the altar, screaming in horror as Ambiorix carved the baby out of her mid-section.

Through a splay of screams, spewing cherry-colored fluid and pulpy gray tissue, Ambiorix performed his duty. Stepping back in a moment with the infant, Ambiorix felt the child contort as more pliable gore fell away.

With his pinkie finger, he cleared the tiny mouth and held the baby up. By means of a scream, the child's tone joined the throng of barbarians now gathered in the inner temple room.

Day of Iniquity

With great happiness, they shouted a welcome to their blood, led in cheers by the clapping niece of the chief, herself sporting a bloody nose and gore staining her blouse. Another cut was made and Ambiorix turned, showing them all. Quickly, word spread that it was a boy. He handed the child to his niece.

"You … bastard…." the celebrant of Alagar stammered, as he glared at the dying woman, who tried to fix her guts back in a few times before the agony overtook her.

Ambiorix watched as his niece removed the upper flap of her chain mail, and then her bloody blouse. With no hesitation, she placed the child to her left breast and it fed. Smiling, she then bowed her head to her uncle and said, "Though this isn't my daughter who died weeks ago, I shall raise him as my son."

"Good," Garretson said as the crowd applauded. "Then he'll not have a mother who tried to sacrifice him to a filthy fuckin' god for gold."

Laughter rippled through the chamber as the priest gaped at the suffering woman. He was about to cut her throat in mercy when Ambiorix slashed at the priest's wrist. The cleric dropped the knife as blood gouted from his forearm.

"No compassion for her," Ambiorix said ruefully. "Let her die as all traitors and the unfaithful must."

The mass of hirsute humanity started to recede from the temple and the priest shouted, "That is it? You are just going to leave?"

"I have what I came for," Ambiorix replied, waving at his son, feeding and mewling at his niece's breast. "My one true love."

"You destroyed all of my magnificent plans, all of my dreams of power at the great day of sacrifice," the priest screamed, fists hitting the altar and the dying woman's head alternately. "I could have beaconed the demons to bestow me proper power, and you slew all of them, all of the other carriers of the seed, for what? For that barbarian bastard?"

Ambiorix stopped, turned and said, "All that matters is blood. Isn't that what all of you rubbish ministers say? Isn't that what all of your demon lords require for happiness? Hell, isn't that what the one, true God really is supposed to desire for the forgiveness of sins--blood? Yet, you find it so hard to understand that we would do all of this for blood. You have not the right to survive."

Leading the old priest to focus on him, Ambiorix walked across the room. With a fast motion, his niece drew back and threw a dagger. End over end, the blade flew true and struck the priest's throat. The old man instinctively removed the blade, tearing loose his Adam's apple. The priest fell, choking and writhing in the dust by the ruined altar of big titties.

They turned their backs on the dead priest and the crying woman. The tribe left the ruins of Larak.

Before they set out for their mountainous home, they stopped at the oasis to water their horses. Again, the old watcher came out of his home to see Ambiorix. This time, the watcher's eyes widened at the sight of the new baby.

"So," the watcher said, pondering the significance of what he saw. "You have found your love that was lost in the ruins at Larak?"

"Yes," Ambiorix proclaimed with pride in his voice. "This is my son; the only thing truly conjured in the day of iniquity wrought at Larak." Buoyant laughter traveled through the crowd. "Let that be a lesson to all, old man. If you try to use blood for blood, the wrong thing may come unto you."

The watcher nodded and stared at the child. "How is this one to be named?"

Ambiorix reached out and his huge hand touched the chest of the boy. Tiny fingers gripped the hand of the warrior, and turned into fists. The bluish green eyes of the baby blinked, and peered up at his father.

"He shall be called Gorias, after my grandfather. The name means, *King of the Bastards*. Born into a world of blood and violence, let him get his mouth full of it. He better get used to it."

The barbarian horde then extolled Wodan to bless Gorias, son of Ambiorix, with life and strength.

Gorias cried out as well to the clear, afternoon sky. The infant studied the blood on his hands. Years later, Ambiorix's niece swore unto Wodan that little *Gorias laughed.*

The End

Ashes of the All-Father

Ashes of the All-Father

"Life is pleasant. Death is peaceful.
It's the transition that's troublesome."
-ISAAC ASIMOV

I-Dreams and the Caravan

Like many Thulites in the antediluvian world, Chief Ambiorix hated magic. His Ingaevone folk in Thule were loath to trust in workers of the black arts outside the unforgiving Zenghaus Mountains. Granted, the Oracle of Wodan, Ivor, and his shamans held the grim secrets of the netherworld, but mostly Thulites kept that sort of thing quiet. Ambiorix, a man of action, preferred to trust in what he could see, even when crossing the Earth to exact a vendetta.

At this particular time, due to such a payback, many of his

rugged tribe lingered, pitching tents in the southeast by a Black Sea far from their home in the icy north. When terrible dreams assailed the Chief's mind, he considered seeing the woman in their tribe that dealt in Oneiromancy. He held back his desire and never shared the dreams with others because of fears all barbarians held; that such visions came by demons or spirits reaching out from beyond.

At least that's what Ambiorix pondered as he drank himself to sleep. Ambiorix also refused to share because of another primitive fear; that his mind might be weakening due to age.

When an imperious voice made requests to him in this dreamtime, Ambiorix ceased to drink before retiring, which amazed his young son Gorias a great deal. However, his abstinence from the concoction of slurry of mashed vegetables failed to silence the voice. The stark, even-tempered tone repeated, night after night. The statements imparted to Ambiorix's savage brow soon led him to new vistas, and showed a peculiar vision.

An imperious face soon formed within his mind to give the voice more horrors. The image remained cloudy, but what this male persona revealed proved clear, taking the Chief to places only seen by birds in the air. He saw, over the rough lands north of Shynar, a line of travelers. Ambiorix recognized certain fashions or diverse folk from his travels, but many of these people were aliens from his culture and the tribe of kidnappers his folks traveled here to butcher.

Ashes of the All-Father

Amidst the groups of camels, horses, carts, and assorted goods in baskets, a man seemed set apart from the rest. This man, a short, older fellow, sported a scarlet glow trimming his frame. The narrator of Ambiorix's myriad dreams said this individual looked as such to make sure Ambiorix didn't miss him. The dialogue of the dream didn't have explain to Ambiorix that the crimson halo blazed to show the calamitous nature for the oldster.

Each night the dreams deepened, and Ambiorix saw this red man, his manner, attributes, and strange body among the others' mundane activities. The way the elder one kept to himself and prayed to unknown spirits, Ambiorix soon named him a necromancer. The left arm of the wizard hung in a sling. The only reason this proved abnormal was that on the night the dreams stopped Ambiorix saw the old man use the fingers as weapons; not as a fighter, but literally ripping them off and throwing them at people. They exploded into cloudy mist and people died as if swatted down by a huge arm.

These images made Ambiorix jerk back into the world of the lucid. Still, he told not his son Gorias, nor his women, of the visions.

The dreams stopped abruptly. Ambiorix believed the revelations an act of a spirit or forces beyond his control. The face often came back to him of the man who spoke the dreams; the perfect, unblemished countenance he would never forget.

The tribe set out to return home, a journey of many months, but then word came that a caravan of goods would pass by the base of the mountain where they camped. Ambiorix flinched, but didn't show concern to his tribe when they put forth the idea of raiding the well-stocked caravan for their trip. Ambiorix reasoned that he hadn't seen any of his own kin in the visions. He also figured that this might be the only way to remove the dire memories from his head, in facing the caravan and whatever it held. Besides, he wasn't afraid to die.

While he looked down on the lumbering caravan, Ambiorix stood with his long-haired tribe and said, "These fools trek across a route hardly well trod. They have no inkling of what terror can fall on them from the mountains. Just a few guards or sleepy pickets to watch for danger, hah, I see they post dwarves for this duty. It makes sense, they're supposed to have keen eyes."

The raid on the trade route along the northern curl of the Euphrates River proved an unabashed success. Certain bandits and bad men lurked in the wilds along any route, but nothing could have prepared those in the train for what thundered out of the Caucaus Mountains. Over two hundred Thulite warriors flooded the caravan and broke the back of the slow-moving train.

Swinging battle-axes, clubs, swords and war-hammers, the wave of howling giants struck the side of the caravan, killing every man and beast that stumbled into their path. Ambiorix led the charge as any chief would, cleaving the head of the first turbaned man who raised his arm in front of him. A spray of brains sent both left and right, the man fell fast as the raiders passed by. They struck the convoy with a broad-sided stroke, and so many died or were wounded in the first wave that pandemonium reigned.

Since they crushed the initial resistance, a few of the younger warriors took to jesting with the fleeing caravan members. One lassoed a trader, but the rope tightened about his neck, not his midsection as the Ingaevone planned. As the raider turned to ride, he dragged the man by the neck for a few yards, and then struck a hump the ground. The force popped the head free, leaving him to drag nothing. Blood spurted into the dirt, much to the hilarity of the Ingaevone children also aiding in the raid.

"They call it obsidian," the leader of the Ingaevone raiders said, pulling a piece of material from an overturned cart. Many looked at Ambiorix as he spoke, and eyed the material. "It'll be good for spear-heads and knives, for it doesn't break as easy as our crude metals."

Many heads turned as a wagon thundered past them. They soon realized two Ingaevone youths drove the wagon, beating the horse into a heavy lather. A twisting, echoing scream wafted from this cart and made Ambiorix squint, curious of its origin. On the rear wheels spun dwarves, spread eagle, obviously affixed there by the boys. Unsure it they were tied or nailed in place, Ambiorix sighed and said to his men, "Tell those boys to quiet down."

Though a few errant arrows flew at them, little in the way of resistance came. Perhaps it was the obvious beaten nature of the caravan's survivors, or the discovery of barrels of beer in one wagon, that made the killing stop.

Two hirsute barbarians carried a man in baggy robes aloft in jest. His tiny legs kicking, he cursed them saltily as they threw him to the ground before their leader. This ruddy-faced man touched a broken, hawkish nose and continued to curse at Ambiorix.

Thick arms folded, Ambiorix listened to him with a bored expression on his bearded face. "Garretson, is there any reason we shouldn't just kill them all?"

Garretson, the stoutest of the warriors acknowledged, "Their women aren't worth having, chief. They look brittle like birds."

"Where are our young ones?" Ambiorix asked his men. "Where are Gorias and the rest?"

The men gestured to the edge of the caravan, at dust billowing up in the noonday's light. Two-dozen youths, all barely over ten years of age, had dismounted and set about smashing the baskets off the camels.

Ambiorix sighed as one of his men set a cart afire nearby. "Children, heh. If they were older, they would've cut the damned cinch strap and stayed on their mounts."

The other Ingaevones laughed and Garretson said, "But that's why they come along at a young age, to learn and experience the world."

"True enough," Ambiorix acknowledged the looming tribesman. He then cast his eyes down toward the smaller man on the ground. "As my son learns the lessons provided by the weak to the strong, is there any reason you can give me why we should spare your miserable lives?"

The look of vile defiance still framed the bloody-faced man's maw, and then suddenly it shifted. His anger faded, and he spewed, "The Elder! You will want to go after him into the city of Urak."

"Elder? Who is this?" Ambiorix wondered with a dubious tone in his voice, a boot balanced on an overturned cart as screams of the vanquished filtered around them.

The small man leapt off the ground and put his hands to the chest of Ambiorix. Since the thuggish barbarian wore no shirt, the only thing for him to grasp was the leather strap across his body that supported the broadsword sheath on his back. At this action, Garretson and others took a step toward them, but Ambiorix showed no fear. He let the little man touch him as he made his case.

"The Elder, the old wizard Hasan, that is who. I am Cyrus, and by Syn I swear that Hasan has great powers he carries, and knows the location of greater booty."

Ambiorix grabbed the little man by his shoulders and pulled him off his person. Lifting the man higher to look him in the eye, Ambiorix asked, "Powers, aye, Cyrus? And what treasure is this that Elder Hasan knows about?"

The man stammered, "He knows where the tomb of the Son of God lies, in all of its riches and splendor."

Ambiorix threw the small man down as if he were so much

trash. Groaning and grabbing his back, Cyrus turned over. Ambiorix said, "Bah, what have I need of a Nephilum's tomb? There are sons of God a-plenty in this wretched world, old man. Giants, petty and boring, they are hard to miss in this age of iniquity. I will go visit the ones I know and trust if I have need to see one in person. Why do you think we live in the mountains?"

Garretson asked eagerly, "Then they all must die, Ambiorix?"

The youths ran up beside Garretson, faces full of dirt and smiles. "Yes, father," the auburn-haired youth Gorias exclaimed. He was a head taller than the other boys were, barely eleven years old. "Let it be death for them, all!"

Ambiorix looked west, in the direction of the city of Urak mentioned by the caravan leader. "Urak, modern city of light, home of more trollops than holy men." This statement caused mirth from the hairy men, and then Ambiorix eyed the voyager. "You try and barter your lives with this information? Why should it matter what happens now that you have said this? I should appreciate your words and spare your life? Why did this Elder Hasan leave your great company anyway?"

When the man fell silent, Garretson offered, "I hear in Jericho they use pain and suffering to make a man talk."

Ambiorix shrugged. "Torment may make some men speak. A dead man says nothing, though."

"Many plotted against him," the Cyrus admitted. "We only learned of his plans when he drank too much."

Ashes of the All-Father

Garretson quipped, "That'll happen."

Cyrus went on to say, "Hasan grew enraged for what he sought had been moved in months past. That's why he was with us. For what he hunted after lay in Urak. He feared we would follow him to the exact spot and try to overtake him for the treasure."

Ambiorix chuckled as the Thulites looked on eagerly. "You sing a peculiar tune, old one. It's almost too crazy to be a lie. One would think a man with his life in the balance would tell a better tale."

"Urak?" one of the men said. "Is that not where the medusa turned half the men into stone?"

Garretson snapped, "That's old woman talk, nothing that will concern a fighting man."

The caravan leader was about to speak when his head snapped to the direction of the son of Ambiorix, Gorias. In the young man's grasp was a bundle of cloth under one arm and a small, jeweled box under the other. Though he tried to face Ambiorix again with a calm face, the chief was no fool. He knelt down and grabbed Cyrus by his baggy robes.

"What is it?" he requested, and then dropped him. Taking just a few strides, he reached his son and took the box from under his arm. The boy looked on with innocence. "Where was this?"

Gorias pointed at the destroyed cart near a broken-legged horse. The animal bleated, as Gorias said, "It was in the back of the cart under many blankets, as if hidden, father."

Ambiorix was about to speak, but the horse shrill annoyed him. "Cut that damned animal's throat, would one of you?" he requested, expecting to be obeyed. "Quarter up the meat for later as well."

"Yes chief," a couple of the Ingaevones said, and departed toward the injured horse.

When silence reigned, Ambiorix studied the box and fiddled with the latch on the front. Easily, the box opened. Ambiorix blinked, and his frown deepened. He showed Garretson, his son, and a few of the men in the area, and then closed the box.

Addressing the traveler, Ambiorix said, "What insanity is this? Did this belong to this Elder Hasan?" All Ambiorix waited for was a nod from the old man before he asked, "What was he, a leper? Why would he leave his pinkie finger in a box in the caravan?"

"Wizards do crazy things, savage," the traveler replied with a mild shrug. "Perhaps he sought the tomb for greater powers to make himself whole again. Hasan was not a well man. His left arm was in a sling. I noticed that he missed fingers."

"At least one," Ambiorix sighed, fighting down tremors induced by the memory of his horrid dreams. He threw the box back into a nearby cart. Gorias' face darkened, wounded at the action that deprived him of a prize, but Ambiorix's stern face glared at him. "There will be better boxes to open soon, boy. I say we go unto the city of Urak and leave these fools to gather themselves up. If we find greater treasure, then we'll go directly back to the mountains. If not, these jackasses cannot repair and scatter away fast as the roaches they act like. We can come back and kill them afterwards."

The Ingaevones seemed disappointed at this, but Ambiorix stepped closer to Garretson and said, "There are great whorehouses at the edge of Urak. That may be enough to quench the thirst of the warriors and continue the education of the boys for now. If not, we'll ride back and slay all those in the caravan for deceiving me." Ambiorix looked at Cyrus. "I'll drag you home until you're bones."

Garretson watched the faces of the boys light up and he asked Ambiorix, "Then you won't pursue the tales of this Elder Hasan?"

Ambiorix raised an eyebrow. "I wasn't lying when I told that runt I had no use for the wiles of a son of God, Garretson. A dead one really has no value I can see. At least they talk less."

When the Thulites mounted up and prepared to leave, the leader of the caravan leaned on a cart and stared at Ambiorix. "You may be mistaken, chief," he said with a wry smile. "It isn't that Elder Hasan seeks any grave, but the body in that grave. That is his treasure, you see. What he seeks is the body of the Son of God itself."

Ambiorix chuckled, legs gripping the sides of his mount. "Then he's a mule and I would be the one trying to ride him in a fancy race if I pursued such a thing."

Cyrus replied, "It isn't just a body, barbarian, and it isn't just any son of God." He paused, pointed to the sky, and declared, "It was the first Son of God."

Garretson reined in his horse next to Ambiorix and grumbled, "Is that old fool still babbling for his life? Should I cut his damned head off as an example? Or, better yet, let Gorias do it? I always like to see how surprised kids get at how much blood comes out at their first beheading."

Ambiorix shook his head from side to side. "Let us be gone from here. I hope we don't have to return. We shall send the larger pieces of booty back up the mountain. The women and wee ones are waiting for us anyway. Those old enough for man-making time will come along unto Urak."

The massive force of raiders left the caravan in pieces. They headed northwest, toward the city of Urak.

The leader of the caravan took a few breaths, coughed violently, and then started laughing.

$$***$$

II-Bloody House

The sight of a whorehouse brings out the bestial nature in most any man. The more savage they are in breeding, the more frenzied this outward reaction becomes. Ambiorix knew that the series of brothels in the outer ring of Urak would be more than enough to quench the hunger of his men. With any luck, it would further the manhood process of the group of youths they brought in tow.

However, the emotion of terror was not one usually associated with a house of prostitution, aside from fear of performance.

The first of Ambiorix's men that went into the whorehouse were swiftly out again. One of them vomited onto the hitching posts. Since this was an older tribesman, the one Garretson had dress and prepare the flesh of the horse for later consumption, this spewing of wine troubled Ambiorix.

"Hold your guts, you men," Ambiorix thundered as he dismounted. Gorias was fast at Ambiorix's heels, off his horse and stalking behind his towering father.

One of the men shouted from the door of the establishment, "Oh, by Wodan, sir, they are undone!" He then vomited near the watering trough, and then in between horses.

Ambiorix grimaced and looked down at Gorias. "Care to lose your breakfast?"

Bright eyed, Gorias shrugged. "I can eat again."

Drawing their swords, Ambiorix, Gorias, and Garretson stepped into the brothel. It was a charnel house, full of female and male bodies, bloody and almost inhuman in their appearance. Eyes were burst asunder, pooled up with gray slime and scarlet ichor; mouths locked in the rigor of a horrid death, almost filled up with blood. Tongues lashing out to heaven for mercy were stilled, locked in rigor of crimson. Several of the men in the houses had vomited their guts out in loops. A few of these dead men had drawn their swords in defense, and still held them tight.

Garretson rubbed his mouth, wondering, "Were some of them guards of the house, or just men in for the night? I wouldn't know a lawman from Urak to see one."

His anger fuming, Ambiorix retorted, "Does it matter now? They all look alike once your guts are on the outside." He looked down at his son. Gorias looked a shade of green, but didn't become sick. "These people have been dead a long time. Look at them. The blood is dry."

A shrilled, weak voice croaked from the next room, "Run away! Flee from the face of foul necromancy!"

Ambiorix and Garretson exchanged a glance as one of the men stepped forward to try and open the door. Quickly, Ambiorix barked, "Don't be a fool! This isn't worth wasting one of our lives over."

Nevertheless, the hulking youth pulled the door open. His tawny hair flew back and he nearly dropped down to his buttocks. From out of the next room fell a man not bloodied by whatever killed the inhabitants of the whorehouse, but his eyes were gouged out. He crawled out slowly, weeping.

"Who are you and why did this happen?" Ambiorix demanded of him, unsure if truth resided in this man.

"The Elder poisoned them all," the man muttered as he crawled on shaky limbs. They backed away from the advance of the slobbering man, as if he was a rat. "That is what the dying ones told me when I came for my weekly visit. What he cursed them with, the evil of his own hand, still was strong enough to make me very ill. However, one of the dying grabbed me in their death rictus and I was trapped here for a day."

"Damn," Ambiorix said, and no other words came. Gorias reached up with his free hand to touch his father's, but the chief pulled away, focused forward.

The man blubbered, "Can you imagine what it is like being in a house of the dead for a day? One of them holding your ankle, too tight to escape?"

"He's mad," Garretson stated the obvious, with a wave of his left hand. "He gouged out his own eyes."

"Exactly," Gorias said with some disdain in his tone. "I would have cut the fingers off the idiot holding me before I went crazy."

Ambiorix patted his son on the shoulder roughly, and then told Garretson, "Why would an old man come into a place like this? For food or shelter? I doubt for the sex, but one never can tell of these old ones."

Garretson replied, "I would say so. It was a long trip from the caravan. It took us all afternoon to reach here. I dunno know if he was on foot or not. I knew we should have strung up that Cyrus in the caravan for more words."

The dying man blurted, "He came for blood! Though he needed sustenance, the Elder satisfied his need for blood by destroying the house with his dismal magic. Through the bloody mess he meted out, he gained what knowledge no man would give. He required blood for his magic."

Ambiorix never looked at the man again, but said to the group of his fighters, "Some wizards divine in blood or intestines. By the look of this place, this Elder got what he wanted to see."

"Did they say where this Elder went?" Garretson asked the man on the floor.

"Marduk," he croaked. "He went unto the Grotto of Marduk."

Many of the Ingaevones blinked and their mouths dropped open at the mention of this spot. Ambiorix scowled at his tribesman as they talked amongst themselves about legends and tales of the grotto. "This man is crazy. Naught else can be gained from talking to him. I'll hear no more discussion of medusas and the Grotto. Those are stories to scare weak children and disturb their dreams." He knelt by the fireplace. The immense hearth was long cold, but it looked as if gray ashes were planted in a burst all over the interior of the structure.

"Are you near the hearth? Don't touch it." the man exclaimed. "That is where he threw his finger of wrath! It blew away into a cloud of ash and all of them died because of it."

Ambiorix didn't touch the strange design. He breathed hardly at all as his dreams crashed back into the front portion of his brain. Ambiorix motioned at Garretson with his head, a sharp nod. With haste, Garretson drilled his sword down into the back of the insane man. The blow nailed the madman's heart and left lung to the floor. In an instant, the man raved no more.

"Marduk indeed," Ambiorix said, bile in his words, as he walked out of the whorehouse.

One of the Ingaevone fighters said to him eagerly, "Chief, it's not necessary to go into town for whores. We can go back unto our mountains. Our own women or our hands will suffice this night."

Another younger warrior stepped up, agreeing with him vigorously.

Ambiorix sighed with disgust, reading the fear in his men at the rumors of the Grotto of Marduk. "A troop of dead sluts does not affect your mettle, but mention Marduk and you all want to run away."

Gorias stepped nearer to his sire. "Isn't the temple of Marduk far south of here?"

"Yes," Ambiorix affirmed, returning his sword behind his back as they returned to the horses. "Ya listened good to the yarns at night before we gutted that village, huh? But Marduk was rumored to have traveled West, and never returned to his peoples. It is his grotto that they all get weak-kneed over, son."

Holstering his short sword at his hip, Gorias said quietly, "I've heard the tales of Marduk and how they steal little girls to satisfy his unearthly lust."

Hand on his saddle, Ambiorix muttered, "People talk too much."

Gorias went on, saying, "They say Marduk eats them after he splits them in half, in his rapture. That's the point of his Grotto, is it not?"

Ambiorix barked at his son, "Do not believe every tale you hear around the hearth."

Gorias showed no hurt by the vile tone Ambiorix used on him. Instead, Gorias asked, "This Elder Hasan seeks after Marduk? Is he the son of God the man in the caravan mentioned?"

For a period, there was silence among them all, and then Ambiorix said, "Marduk was not the first son of God, nor even one of the first sired by the Angelic or Demonic host."

Scratching his beard, Garretson put out, "I know what you're thinking, Ambiorix, but those tales are older than children stories around the campfire."

Ambiorix frowned at him, speaking softly. "Yes, but they have a grain of truth."

Gorias spoke up, "Unlike the fireside tales?"

The tall man reared back, prepared to strike his son. Gorias stood still, ready for the blow and closed his eyes. Ambiorix dropped his hand and said, "You're correct, son. There are many truths amongst the lies in tales spun to children." As the group thinned out around the horses, Ambiorix grabbed his son and bent so that only the child could hear him. "Next time, do not seal your eyes when expecting a blow. Stare into the face of your fate like a man. Don't ever let me think I sired a daughter, not the way you fight."

Clenching his midriff belt, Garretson looked toward the nearby city and said, "I wonder if all of the brothels of Urak are like this?"

Ambiorix looked at the other boys and said, "Do not let this dissuade you from whorehouses, lads. There are plenty of good whores in the world."

Gorias nodded. "I believe you, father."

$$***$$

III-Trail of the Elder

Following the path taken by the Elder Hasan proved quite easy. One need not be a skilled tracker to follow a trail of dead bodies. Every place they stopped, a boarding house, another brothel, or a hostel-saloon, lifeless bodies abounded. Sometimes on the road there was a fetid corpse, a lodging to a host of flies, locked in strange rigor, as if they fought their demise heartily. However, in each location, the mass murder took on a different guise. For example, in the boarding house and stable, everyone was dead of a swelling at their necks, oozing black fluid from all orifices. In the next brothel, thousands of sores discharging puss covered the flesh of each person, customer and whore alike.

Ambiorix noted that the tavern they visited was lightly

populated, probably in conjunction with the high concentration of common people in the brothel. Those deceased in this establishment were drenched in sweat, and left cold with their eyes open.

Each stop the Ingaevones made caused more men to suggest they return home and stop this trek. Ambiorix released a few at a time, instructing them to meet up at the border of Urak, but not to return home just yet.

Garretson gazed at a man by the side of the road, drowned in his own vomit, and suggested, "Ambiorix, no good can come of this. There is naught to gain by pursuing a man who leaves this much death in his wake."

Ambiorix frowned and gazed into Urak proper. "True. We owe this city nothing by stopping the Elder Hasan." He faced Gorias and a few of the other youths, reading them well. While they seemed perplexed by the departed men, none wore a guise of fear. Ambiorix lowered his voice to Garretson and said, "I also see nothing to stop this old man from slaying us in such a manner, should we encounter him. I see a pattern, any fool can."

No longer showing his randy nature, Garretson nodded. "Yes, foolish to come this far, chief."

Hands turning to fists, Ambiorix leered at him. "I need your counsel, not your scourging, Garretson. My father died long ago."

As the group mounted up and encircled Ambiorix in the street, Gorias let his mount drift towards Urak, looking down the streets.

"Boy, heed your father," Garretson said, waving for him to join them.

Still fascinated by something, Gorias never flinched. The warriors looked at the boy and no one moved to join him.

Ambiorix commanded in a strong voice, "Son? Gorias! What is it?"

"Look, father," he slowly raised an arm and pointed, his manner almost pensive. "You see the statues on either side of the street?"

Indeed, they noted humanoid shapes across the street from each other near to various town buildings. Gorias' horse trotted in the vicinity of them, and many Ingaevones joined Ambiorix in following the boy.

"What is it?"

Gorias pointed down the avenue, saying, "The path of the medusa victims is clear enough. Look at them. These were not carved by man."

Stroking hair on the back of his head with nervousness, Garretson looked at the stone figures, and admitted, "Damn cruel stone cutter if they were, boy. Medusas? Gorgons? Wodan forbids it!"

Truly, the shapes appeared dissevered from white rock. Yet, each human was not posing, or looking off stoic, after a heroic deed. These figures stood locked in an expression of horror, afraid, eyes bulging, and mouths agape.

A few of the warriors started to disengage, clearly disturbed by what they saw. They stopped short of fleeing, looking to Ambiorix for orders.

Eyes full of resignation, mind afire with his past dreams of terror, Ambiorix said, "We must go. This isn't our home or our place to stop this kind of evil."

With youthful glee, Gorias exclaimed, "Father, are these really the work of gorgons? They really do exist! Did they once pass by here?"

Ambiorix jabbed one of the statues with his boot, causing a bit of the stone to chip away from the human figure's forearm. "These look to be well weathered. Look closely, son, if these were indeed men turned to stone by the gorgons, it was a very long time ago. If they did, they are the opposite of the sons of god that old man Hasan seems to desire so much."

Garretson looked down the avenue. "The lords of Urak keep these in the street as a reminder, you figure?"

Shrugging, Ambiorix reined in his horse and declared, "Perhaps. I care not for this vagueness. No treasure can be worth any of this death or dancing so close to the jests of the gods."

The boy looked at the stone shapes. His eyes never blinked. "Where do the gorgons come from, father?"

Ambiorix spat and said dismissively, "It depends on which lying tongue one listens to, son. Some say they are revolting creatures bred by some demon, while others have a grimmer origin."

Facing his father, Gorias asked, "What is it?"

Boots shifting in his stirrups, Ambiorix sighed. "You know of the sons of the gods, the Nephilum giants? They are all huge, powerful men, correct?"

Gorias nodded.

Ambiorix posed to him, "It ever strike you as odd that the angelic or demonic host never fathered a female child from the womb of an earth woman?"

Mouth agape, Gorias took a few moments before saying, "Wodan's beard! The gorgons..."

Reining his horse away from Urak, Ambiorix stated, "Which is why they cannot breed with men, and the males who try, freaks are born. The Curse gets deeper the farther the bloodline strains. Let us begone from this place."

"Father," Gorias whispered, again pointing into the city. "That must be the Grotto of Marduk!"

With some violence in his motions, Ambiorix yanked his mount away from the others and joined his son. He leaned over and grabbed Gorias by his outstretched arm and said quietly, "Listen, you young mule, trust the words of your father and let us depart from here."

Gorias and the rest stared at the stone building as a startled cry split the night. Before any of the stunned men could stop him,

Gorias kicked his horse and bolted toward the Grotto of Marduk and where they heard the scream.

***

ACT IV—Grotto of Marduk

Ambiorix kicked his horse, cursing. He followed his son through the dirt streets and towards the stone building devoted to Marduk. If anyone watched as Ambiorix's mount kicked up the town's dirt road, they didn't emerge from their homes or buildings to make it obvious. Still, he felt eyes on him, either from this world or another.

If anything, the Grotto resembled a figure eight, with two circular structures intersecting at the middle. The Grotto looming like three homes had been stacked atop each other, constructed only of concise bricks. Each stone bore hand-scribed decorations with intricate carvings too small to appreciate from a distance, but, by the bizarre reflection of the torches outside, no two of the polished links were the same.

Gorias had quickly dismounted and ran toward the edifice. The youth stopped, though, and his father caught up with him. Not all of the youthful bravado in the world would make him charge up a railing into a religious site, where a dozen women lay outside, still twitching in death.

With great violence, Ambiorix boxed Gorias' ears from

behind and the boy staggered. A handful of his hair, he turned Gorias around. Pointing in his face, Ambiorix roared, "I will not be disobeyed by a damned pup, even my own." Ambiorix then thought better of his loud tone, scanning the area as his voice echoed.

Though blood trickled from his left ear, Gorias stood tall and faced his father. Truly, the youth was ready to take the next punishment.

Ambiorix frowned, glared down at the dying women, and released him. "Be not so rash, boy, as to rush headlong into your death. It'll find you in its own sweet time."

Gorias pointed at the nearest woman, as a few started to crawl toward them, and said, "Father, they wear robes and finery, their faces are painted as if high born whores." Indeed, the samite gowns trimmed with gold belonged only on the wealthy or those dressed for a purpose. "What are they doing here at a temple of a god?"

After a shove to the right shoulder forced Gorias to walk back from the steps, Ambiorix said, "They are brides of Marduk, adorning in their best cote-hardie gowns. They all wear hemmin veils, see? They go forth into the temple, I hear tell, to have him deflower them of their virginity."

Flabbergasted, Gorias waved at the women as they bled from their mouths and gargled on crimson. "Who kidnapped such a group for this evil thing?"

"No one," Ambiorix sighed, though remaining on guard.

"They desired this duty themselves. No one compelled them. Each volunteered, to break one so pure for the god Marduk."

Hands trembling, mouth working, and no words appearing, Gorias was flustered at the idea of it all. At last he spoke, saying, "This Nephilum, this Marduk should die, father."

Amused by his son's scarlet anger, Ambiorix asked, "Why? You think what he does evil?"

"I don't know if it is evil," said Gorias, eyes burning in the evening like suns. "But it cannot be right."

Ambiorix laughed shortly. "By who's measuring stick?"

Gorias gritted his teeth and gripped his sword handle. "Mine!"

The auburn-haired youth ran up the steps, dodging dead women like a boy in a game, ignoring his father's commanding voice.

Ambiorix's heart boiled in his chest, admiring the child's pluck, yet wanting to beat him bloody at the same instance.

Gorias hit the entrance to the grotto, somewhat stunned that the heavy wooden door of polished wood actually gave way under his weight. Gorias never saw what his father did; that the handle was off. Ambiorix barely had time to note the metal handle, melted like candle wax, before he jumped for his son.

Ambiorix caught Gorias and they went flying through a set of velvety curtains. No floor came up to greet them as they tumbled down stone steps. The boy cried in pain and Ambiorix swore, but when they both realized where they were, and what was happening, they fell silent. Any bruises from their fall would be the least of their worries.

Countless candles and a few stylish tin lanterns lit the large circular chamber. They had no trouble seeing the two huge, musclebound men in white loincloths facing off against a smaller figure. These substantial men sweated heavily, shaven bodies gleaming in the candlelight. Between them stood a slender woman, also with a shaven head, but wearing a spare white tunic that barely covered her midsection.

Clothed in a dusty cloak and cowl, the small man cursed at the three opposing him. The words weren't slang for dung or sexual copulation. Rather, they held the names of demons, and what the shouter wanted them to do to his opponent's mothers.

Still on the floor, Gorias curled into his father's arms and whispered, "The Elder Hasan?"

The old one looked at them, but never reacted in anger or fear. If anything a twisted smile played on the lips of the withered man as he reached toward his left arm. This limb, in a sling as if broken, shone chalky white. Hasan gripped his left ring finger and ripped it off, a savage grin shining in his beard. Only dust dropped from the point of removal and the old one made a fist with his right hand.

The bald woman glared at Hasan with terror in her face, and cartwheeled away from her servants.

Rearing back, the Elder cast a fragment of the finger, now mostly dust, at the large bald man to his right. As the man reacted to the dust in his face, arms up, Hasan repeated the motion towards the other man, with a more backhand swipe.

In unison, the two servants of Marduk started to scream in a higher-pitched tone than Ambiorix thought possible for these thuggish brutes. "They must be Eunuchs," he muttered, starting to pull Gorias to his knees and looking for the door.

However, Hasan and the two screaming men kept moving around the circle, blocking Ambiorix and Gorias' departure. The two Eunuchs inadvertently obstructed their escape as they fell into fits. Their flesh seemed to sprout hives, and they scratched themselves bloody.

Hasan lost concern with the two struggling men and raised his right arm to point at the bald woman. Her lips peeled into a snarl as her hands raised and glowed. She threw a ball of light at Hasan, but it seemed to drop at his feet, off target. The ball unraveled, showing itself to be a large, burgundy-colored spider. Another projectile from the priestess of Marduk also missed Hasan, as if an invisible shield protected him. This ball bounced, hit one of the Eunuchs, and transformed into a scorpion. It struck the big, bloody man, and he shouted even more.

"You cannot overcome my mind," Hasan sneered at her. "Give me what I desire and I shall go."

"You cannot have him," the priestess screamed, retreating toward another velvety curtain across the room. "Through him we will gain even more power."

Ashes of the All-Father

Ambiorix looked at the windows, all incredibly narrow and not large enough to fit a barbarian through. He retreated away from Hasan fast, pulling his son by the elbow and scalp.

Hasan laughed and pointed with his right hand. "You should never have removed him from his resting place, you witch. I claimed him first, so he is mine. Your biggest mistake was not making sure I was dead back in Chanoch."

The priestess' hands smoldered and she snarled, "That's true, old conjure-man. I shall remedy my mistake!"

Ambiorix and his son kept retreating, but were running out of space. The dueling magicians never acknowledged them. Ambiorix wanted to make a quick break for the door, but saw the dead bodies of the Eunuchs criss-crossed on the steps and thought better of the action. If he fell or stepped wrong, it would be their doom.

Hasan retorted to the woman, "Your powers cannot touch me once my mind is focused. Go on, try again."

Once more, she slashed at the air, throwing orbs of luminosity at the Elder. Again, they fell to his feet. One glob changed into a large hornet and the other into an ivory colored cockroach. Neither creature could penetrate the power of the Elder.

Gorias hissed, "We are doomed, father!"

Ambiorix grabbed him by the throat so hard the boy could not breathe. With great power in his tone, but a hardly audible voice, Ambiorix declared, "We are still alive, boy, and there's always a chance if that's so."

Suddenly, the two Thulites couldn't maneuver anywhere else. They were very near to the next curtain, the area where the priestess seemed intent to guard. She faced them and her eyes blazed. Hands radiant, she reared back.

Ambiorix stood and roared, determined to die fighting, great sword off his back and in his hand.

When she cast her spheres of light at him, he parried the balls away, but the impact on his sword sent the heavy weapon flying. Gorias stood up beside his disarmed father and saw the woman's hands flame again.

Ambiorix saw what the priestess did not. Even as she prepared to attack the barbarians, Ambiorix noticed Hasan grinning. He beheld the elderly man break off another joint from one of his petrified fingers and reach back to throw.

Ambiorix grabbed his son and dived through the curtains. As he tumbled into the next dimly-lit chamber, he heard the priestess scream. Truly, Hasan had her dead to rights. Hurriedly trying to find an escape route, and coming up empty, Ambiorix feared the Elder had them dead as well.

"But he doesn't want us," Ambiorix muttered, looking at the center of the chamber.

He saw the same thing that Hasan did when he entered the room; the stone form of Marduk, the Nephilum created by an interbreeding with the demonic host. A giant of nearly nine feet in height, Marduk lay back in repose, naked. His rigid manhood was rendered in a curve, aiming at his head, but away from his flesh.

"Where have you hidden the first Son of God?" Hasan asked calmly, not addressing anyone. He looked the chamber over, and then focused on the rock outline of Marduk. Under him was a platform, or so it appeared, of rectangular stone. Hasan knelt by the box and knocked on it with his knuckles. "So transparent are you fools," he mumbled. He stood and ran his good hand under the lip of the platform that held the shape of Marduk.

Ambiorix held his breath and looked at the drapes. Fifteen feet away, he did not like his chances.

Hasan bent, then pushed up on the lip of the platform, grunting. Exhausted, he stepped back. Frustration filled his curses. Abruptly, he looked at them and said, "You! Barbarians! Help me with this effort."

"What say you?" Ambiorix stammered, surprised by the request.

"All of my power cannot lift this weight, nor can I melt the stone away without damaging what lies inside. You see this thing here, the form of Marduk? This was not carved by the hand of any man. Come closer, savages, see the result of a bastard son of the gods trying to mate with one of his half sisters, a gorgon. He was turned to stone as he drove into her." He gestured at the erect member of stone. "It still breaks the virgins who volunteer to be the vassal for their god."

"Wodan," Gorias whispered, eyes large and focused on the story Hasan told.

"You see the little gutters under him that lead down to the chalice?" the Elder questioned, as he pointed. "That is to catch the fresh virgin blood for sacrifice."

Though they did come closer, Ambiorix still eyed the door. "It's an abomination," Ambiorix said plainly.

Hasan tilted his head to one side and sniffed. "I care little for their practices, either, savage. They have hidden what I want under the plate here. I cannot lift it. Help me elevate this."

Ambiorix didn't answer, still stunned.

Hasan looked grim. "Shall I put this in terms you can comprehend? Help me or I will kill you both."

His shock faded, Ambiorix smirked. "I think you shall slay us anyway."

Hasan pointed to the other room. "There is gold and jewels aplenty out there, now unguarded by the Eunuchs. You can have it all, for that isn't why I'm here. Just aid me and you can go. Wait any more, and I will kill your son to see if that makes you progress faster."

Ambiorix frowned and reached under the lip of the platform holding Marduk. He then switched, placing his shoulders under it, pushing up with his back. Stone ground on granite, and the edge moved.

"Yes," Hasan seethed with great anticipation. "You are doing it, barbarian. What strength you have!"

Unsure if the act would save them, Ambiorix put all of his

power into removing the lid. Shoving it across and then up, the weight tilted and he raised the platform. Marduk turned as if rolling over in bed, and tumbled off. Free of the weight that crashed to the stone floor, Ambiorix flew up from the ground, tossing the plate into the air. It flipped over and landed on Marduk, smashing like glass.

Hasan and Gorias moved in different directions; Hasan back a bit, and then forward, and Gorias around the side, near the impact point of the lid.

Sucking air and turning to face the result of his labors, Ambiorix again eyed the curtains, but for a moment. Since his son was out of arms' reach, his first instinct vanished. Soon, he found himself stepping closer, beside the Elder Hasan, peering into the oblong container. Serving as a pedestal for Marduk's deflowering center, the stone box was a repository for a secret of the dark priesthood.

"What is that?" Ambiorix found himself asking, not believing his own words.

Hasan's portentous eyes widened, as the faint luster filled the box. "Look onto that face, so sculpted and perfect. See the ultimate face of humanity, barbarian? That is the face of perfection, and the ultimate visage of clay come alive."

The illuminated figure looked like a statue, but not in the same manner of Marduk. If anything, these manly figures appeared almost animated, yet covered in a fine layer of dust.

"This is what you desire?" Ambiorix asked, not knowing what to think of the likeness in front of him; save for it was the exact image from his dreams that spoke to him.

Hasan carried no malice in his manner or words as he said, "Yes, this is the first son of God himself, barbarian; the man formed of the dust of the ground, with the ultimate God's own hands. This is Adam, his own self."

Ambiorix's eyes narrowed. "He wasn't afflicted by the gorgons, was he?"

Hasan grinned. "You are a clever man, savage. Adam is dead. He died long ago naturally, and his form has yet to rot. You see, we all will meet our fate in the earth, all of us will return to the clay of creation. With this one, he is trifling a bit longer. His flesh was meant to last forever. Perhaps the Creator has trouble letting go of such a perfect face, eh?"

Ambiorix stepped back one pace, but never ran. "I care not for the value you place in a dead body."

Hasan smiled, not looking at Ambiorix. "I grant you life, barbarian. While bloodthirsty in my trade, I can be magnanimous in victory. Take your boy and go. The purposes for this great magic will be known to you in time."

Ambiorix turned to look, and didn't see his son until it was too late. The Elder's face contorted just as a sickening pop resonated in the chamber. Frozen in place, Hasan shivered, and then his body lost control. His sphincter let go, as his left arm fell from his sling, turning to powder as it bounced on the stone floor.

Gorias stepped into view, holding the article he drove into the skull of the Elder; the broken-off stone member of Marduk. Gorias stepped closer to the Elder, and whispered in his ear, "You are wrong, swine, I'm not a boy." He stabbed the stone bludgeon into the skull of the old man once again, and this time brains spewed into the box. "I am a man." Gorias then grabbed the Elder by the buttocks and threw him into the stone box. A cloud of dust erupted from inside and Ambiorix yanked his son back. As the debris settled, they both peeked inside.

The body of Adam, the all-father, was no more. Only a pile of dust and the corpse of the Elder Hasan remained inside.

Ambiorix looked at his son. Gorias smiled, content with his actions. Slapping the rock phallus from his son's grip, Ambiorix grabbed him by the forearm and they left the inner sanctum of Marduk.

While Gorias looked back, Ambiorix did not. It was not the body of Adam, the man rumored to father all of humanity, that disturbed the barbarian. Ambiorix never confessed what made him afraid; the fact that Adam was missing his left arm.

***

Epilogue

While Ambiorix and Gorias stayed outside the Grotto, the chief told Garretson and the rest to sack the first chamber of Marduk. "If you go beyond the curtain, I cannot guarantee your life," Ambiorix warned. "I do not plan to load my mount up with great riches."

Garretson laughed, and then asked, "Why is this?"

Ambiorix looked into the distance, as if he could see the person on his mind in the darkness. "Because I want the horse to have fresh legs when we catch up to the caravan. I want this horse to have plenty of balls left, when I drag that little bastard from the caravan to death."

However, Ambiorix did not attain this desire. When they caught up with the caravan the next day, they found them all dead, consumed by a plague that made their intestines loop from their jaws. The Thulite chief settled for spitting on Cyrus's dead body before they left. From the trail of bodies, it was obvious where the problem emanated from.

That night, when they lay down to sleep, Ambiorix imagined the finger of Hasan bursting, and slaying the entire caravan in their absence.

Covering his mighty frame from the chill, Ambiorix dropped into a deep slumber.

He did not dream.

THE END

Author and Finisher of Our Flesh

Author and Finisher of Our Flesh

"Life isn't fair. It's just fairer than death, that's all."
-WILLIAM GOLDMAN

Have a care, Hjordis," the burly soldier near the door of the tavern cautioned another who sported the stallion insignia of the Transalpinian military. "It isn't wise to taunt the largest man in the bar."

Hands on his lean hips, Hjordis grinned through a neatly cut goatee at the red haired man who spoke, then back at the hirsute individual at the corner table. This huge man, who weaved in his chair due to the effects of the empty flagons of whiskey around him, appeared in his own world, muttering names, his long mane of hair twitching as he drummed gnarled fingers. Though his cloak lay twisted askew across the chair to his left, the rough warrior clearly wore intricately plated armor, sporting a blue tinge.

Steven Shrewsbury

"Why worry about this one, General Thynnes?" Hjordis asked with arrogance in his tone, chin raised. "We come to recruit the fabled Ingaevone warrior Gorias, the King of all Bastards, and all we find is a big drunk, too soused to hold a sword, much less use one. He looks fallen from his days as a Lord."

Thynnes' right hand remained on the pommel of the blade affixed to his belt as he looked at the shaky figure. In the smoky bar, the former and current taunts of Hjordis made the eyes of the Ingaevone snap up with attentiveness and aim toward them. Though a soldier his entire life, and in the company of the King's champion, Thynnes' stomach churned at the wolfish eyes of the well traveled mercenary, Gorias. The Ingaevones' armor was blood-stained, and the boots grinding the floorboards of the tavern gaped at the edges, well-worn from travel. Thynnes refused to let his guard down.

Hjordis threw back his brown hair and laughed before saying, "I bet you a skin of wine he cannot even get those famous swords off his back, he's so drunk." At his words, several patrons looked from side to side and moved away from Gorias.

Thynnes mused, "The blades that came from Angel's wings? His armor flailed from the flesh of a wyrmling dragon?"

"I've heard the ballads, too, Thynnes. This is the famed fighter from the Caucaus Mountains, slayer of Akhensobek of Kemet, deflowerer of a thousand virgins?"

"Have a care," said Thynnes, his free hand on his white beard.

Author and Finisher of Our Flesh

"We came to enlist his aide, not to incur his wrath."

With a savage snarl, Hjordis proclaimed, "I'm enough to lead this force into the outer lands unto the gate of the Elder Gods, not some reputed warrior from the campfires. The King of Transalpina wasn't wise to send us here." The clientele of the tavern drew a breath and the bald bar tender blinked, mouth open at the proper fighter. The champion roared back, "Shut up, you pansies! I'm the nephew of the bloody King, I am! I'll prove my worth and kill these children of Cthulhu that threaten to assail us…"

From the mouth of the drunken Ingaevone came the slurred words, "Cthulhu can kiss my hairy ass…him and all of his children… what's the worst he can do, kill me?" Then a chuckle echoed in the enormous chest covered by plates of dragon skin armor. At his words, even more of the regulars exited the area near Gorias. Those that enjoyed the hearth nearby also fled.

Hjordis stared at the drunk, seeing Gorias' face almost obscured by wild auburn hair littered with gray, a bushy beard and unkempt mustache. "What say you, lush? How did you get so far north unto refined Albion across the channel from our fair Transalpina? Fighting more wars for money or suckling that bitch queen of the Prytens?"

"Why should I tell a punk like you?" Gorias replied, his words sloppy and falling like wet footsteps. "I'll cut your balls off and feed them to your mother."

To this, Hjordis laughed, but Thynnes didn't.

Gorias wore a feral grin, saying, "But by the looks of you, they've been in her mouth before."

Hjordis' rage exploded and he drew his khopesh. Not a fool, and well aware of the tales of Gorias, the young champion held his ground.

He never had long to wait, for the massive figure jumped into a standing position, sending the table and depleted drinks flying. Hjordis would've lost the bet with Thynnes, for Gorias could unsheathe the twin swords from his back. Boots planted firm, the Ingaevone looked the picture of his legendary fury on the battlefields and bedrooms. However, he took two steps, staggered and fell hard into the next table before Hjordis, busting it into two even pieces. Releasing his gleaming swords, the huge man rolled over and faced up, letting loose a cough, whiskey dripping from his lips. His bleary eyes stared up into the legs of the champion of Transalpina as trembling hands reached up, then fell flat to his heavy waist belt.

With another laugh, Hjordis said, "This is the grand fighter of the ages? Ha! This will truly add to my..."

Whatever Hjordis planned to say was lost in a high-pitched scream, as Gorias's right hand darted up between the young man's legs. The Ingaevone pulled a small dirk from his belt and quickly jabbed it into Hjordis' groin. With a twist of his thick wrist, Gorias destroyed the manhood of the King's champion forever. A splash of crimson spewed from between Hjordis' legs as he dropped his sword and took a single, quivering step. Blood covered Gorias' face, and he never acknowledged its presence. Thynnes read hilarity in Gorias' expression as Hjordis screamed, clutching a ruined crotch.

Gorias sat up like a shot, head impacting with Hjordis backside, sending him tumbling over, sprawling into the seat Gorias just occupied. Gorias moved slowly, climbing to his knees, and took up his swords. Scarlet drops fell from Gorias' nose and chin as he leered at Thynnes. The aged General, red hair faded to ivory, far older than Hjordis, showed his wisdom and a lack of concern for his fellow soldier. He held his ground and never drew steel at the man with blood running from his face. Gorias turned from him and rose to his feet.

"True, I'm older now," muttered Gorias, voice still thick with drink. "Nearly six hundred years have I trod this miserable planet and still, I run into little pukes that want to die more than they want to screw." Gorias gripped his sword pommels and raised his weapons, unsteady in his stance. "You don't have to look me in the eye, fool. Look on forward. Die like the bitch you are." The great swords fell, penetrating the chain mail under shirt, burying themselves in Hjordis' spine. The blades lodged there and caused the champion's right leg to spasm. Gorias cursed and pulled up the swords, carving the champion of Albion open almost to Hjordis' neck. A boot on the younger man's thigh, Gorias pulled the blades from Hjordis and let the dead man fall away.

Many peeking in the bar windows clapped their hands or

slammed the drinks they took with them down in approval at the action. Several stood near the hallway leading to the back door. Thynnes pondered that here in Albion, they found it funny as hell anyone would slay the champion of the Transalpinan folks, their natural enemies, so easily.

Gorias holstered one of the swords, stumbled to the bar, grabbed a flagon of wine that a hefty patron suddenly wanted nothing to do with. He raised it high, toasting, saying, "Wodan takes the piss out of the Elder Gods every day." He drank deep then lowered his head and mumbled, "Wodan pisses on me." Gorias then turned to Thynnes, and grinned, face still painted with the blood of Hjordis' groin and fresh flowing red wine. Gorias then fell to his knees, dropping both his swords and the drink. He took a few strides on his knees as Thynnes left the spot where he stood. Gorias soon fell at Thynnes feet. He rolled over and moaned, "Jenna..." and passed out.

The bar tender and many others applauded again. While Thynnes wore a frown, the barkeep asked him, "Should I summon the constables or the palace guard?"

Hands on his belt, Thynnes gave a heavy sigh as he looked at the prostrate form of Gorias and the corpse of the King's champion. "No. I'll summon my soldiers."

***

Gorias awoke from salty spray in his face and to the weight of heavy chains on his limbs. Panic set in at first, but he felt a strange sense of calm spread over his mind. The open air did that to most Ingaevones. Rolling over, he wasn't tethered down to the small rear deck of the ship as it bounced in heaving blue waters. He flipped over again, not of his own power, smashing into the side guard of the ship.

"Good, you're awake," came the rough voice of Thynnes to Gorias' ears. "That's why I had you brought up from the hold, to see if the sea would bring you around."

Gorias flexed his arms in the chains and tried to brace himself as the long ship dipped low. The columns of stout men rowing to either side of the vessel proved skilled, for they knew how to work in tandem with the rising and falling of the ship. A slender blonde man wearing the Transalpinan Stallion insignia on his loose fitting gypon steered the vessel, probably a drakkar, Gorias guessed, from the side sector. The waters that did spray over the sides missed the men as their rhythm dictated they swayed in another direction. Rolling over from the force of the drop, Gorias looked down the center path of the ship that ran between the rowers, then again at the man who steered, standing to the side of the ship.

"Wodan's ass, where are we?" Gorias wondered, eyes blinking several times.

"The seas, north of Albion, beyond the Pryten wilderness, even east of the Asgardian realm."

Gorias stared, trying to claw at the boards under him. "But

there's naught but the edge of the Earth in that place." He spun again and cursed. "What am I doing here?"

Thynnes grinned, his stark teeth showing through his white beard. "You are in the process of escaping."

"What say you?"

Thynnes motioned to one of his men. "Bekan? Free him." He then said to Gorias. "The chains only bound you to keep you stable in the hold. I over estimated how much of the potion to give you in the holding cell. Perhaps it interacted with the whiskey in your guts, and that is why you slept so long."

As Bekan helped Gorias out of the cumbersome chains, Gorias eyed the young man in Transalpinan soldier's leathers. "I recall a dungeon, a dank place..."

Thynnes nodded as he held onto the rear railing. "Yes, that was your home for a time after word seeped out about Hjordis."

Gorias tried to steady himself on the deck, but his boots slid. He ran both hands across his face and then to his hair. "Hjordis, I remember now." He then glared at Thynnes. "Why am I here? I should be dead or in torture for that."

"You are dead," Thynnes said with a wink. "You died in your sleep and were thrown to the sea. That's what the King of Transalpina believes."

"But Hjordis was kin to the King, a compatriot of yours?"

Nostrils flaring, Thynnes said, "He was a prick, even if he was my future brother in law. You did Albion a favor, Ingaevone. The world is better off without him." He paused and gave Gorias a dour look. "My world, anyhow. Let us go below, Gorias."

The two men went to the hold under the deck of the heaving ship. There was barely room for the two big men to recline across from each other in the cramped quarters of the General.

Thynnes said, "Better to talk here out of the elements and away from the men. They are my loyal soldiers, but I cannot risk a loyalist to the crown betraying me. We are in a proper place to dispose of such a jackass, though."

As he attempted to get comfortable on the gunnysacks behind him, Gorias said, "You have no anger I slew this champion of the King? I see. I saved you the trouble, didn't I?"

With a shrug, Thynnes said, "Yes, you did. We were off on this mission to Kalaallisut for his Majesty Peverall to solve a riddle, anyhow. Your sword is as good as our champion's any day, once you sober up. At least it better well be. Plus, after this mystery is solved, I have other matters in mind."

"You gave me a potion to get me out of the dungeon?" Gorias blinked, attempting to reason everything together. He smoothed down his wild beard as he said, "Then drag my ass all the way to Hyperborea?" Gorias shook his head and even slapped his mane of auburn hair a few times. "I recall the prison...but why? You want me in your debt? I must warn you, the threat of death to me or execution is not that daunting anymore."

Thynnes nodded. "I've heard you are losing your zest for life.

The bards sing tales and stories are told, Gorias. I like the ones where you are younger and kill all the whores in the Irem brothel."

"You can't please everyone, General." Gorias thought for a moment. "Besides, those women were all under the spell of a damned wizard. I could care a fart in a fighting helmet what the bards say." Gorias reflected for a moment before saying, "I once knew a man who claimed to be from beyond Hyperborea from a land called Zobna. He told drunken tales of a volcano at the top of the Earth, of a place called Yaanek or was it Yarak? I get all of that Cthulhu myth ass backwards." Gorias' voice trailed off and he sighed heavily. "They say a god is imprisoned up there. Hell, there's always a god someplace, huh? I forget his name."

Thynnes chuckled and then turned serious. "I'd love to hear all of your tales in time, Gorias, son of Ambiorix."

At his father's name, Gorias' eyes snapped to attention. He remained silence, though. This General knew much about him, indeed.

"However, I have my own plans. I want to kill the King of Albion after this present task concludes."

"Yeah?" Gorias snorted. "Good for you. Most kings should hang."

"I don't want my baby boy Javan growing up near a realm ruled by a freak like Silex, King of Albion, no matter how educated and erudite the society is getting to be. I have daughters a-plenty and one son. I have enough to worry on besides what sort of society they will have to find husbands in."

"Yeah, I've heard of that King, that he fancies little boys as well as goats, Siamese twins and the lot, but I thought those were just ribald bar tales."

Thynnes grimaced. "I wish that was so, but the truth is grimmer still. However, my strategies are growing amongst the few men I could trust. You killing the champion removed one obstacle from my path. I must carry out duties for my sovereign, though, before my trap can be sprung."

Gorias coughed and gave him a nod. "You fancy yourself a suitable replacement for Silex? Best of luck with that."

Thynnes took a flask from his over cloak and unscrewed the cap. "Eh, there would be a knife waiting for my back in time. I haven't worked all the details out just yet. Hell, I even was even willing to get the champion on the Albionese throne and pull his strings, since I lead all of the military. By Rhiannon, that'd be a joke on the old rapist."

Gorias extended his hand and demanded the flask. Thynnes gave it over. Gorias drank a swig. "Hard to live with yer hand up a man's ass, though."

"True," Thynnes conceded and took the flask back. He drank again, then said, "But I need muscle, a new leader that men will follow."

"Damn, I shoulda died in the whorehouse at Irem or with the pirates at Transalpina. So, you want me to kill this King of yours?"

Again, he demanded the container. Again, Thynnes handed it over to him.

"If you like," Thynnes said with a hearty laugh. "That's a matter for another day."

"What was all that blather about children of Cthulhu?"

"We're going to this godforsaken realm to see what has befallen a colony of Albion farmers at the edge of Kalaallisut at Brattahlid. We've sent many knorrs with supplies, then drakkars full of men to see what befell these others. Still, no word came, save for one drakkar that returned with one man aboard."

Gorias looked around. "One man piloted one of these big bastards? Now who is stroking who?"

Thynnes shook his head from side to side as he took the flask of wine back. "No, the gods sailed him back to us."

"The gods have a shitty sense of humor."

"By luck or design, he returned to us. The young man, a sometimes rower and infantry man called Vilborg, was mad as could be, though in the arms of Rhiannon. He told a tale that a great giant lives in the land he visited, coming from north of the settlement. Vilborg said this giant could eat men whole and crap out children of Cthulhu."

While he rubbed a series of scars on his furrowed forehead, Gorias smiled. "Now who is the drunk?"

Casually, Thynnes related, "The kid was mad and had to be put down. No poultice could be made for his mind. Anyway, King Peverall

Author and Finisher of Our Flesh

has sent his stoutest men on this journey. We are just to see what's there, but not get ourselves killed. Many in Transalpina lost family members who have never returned from this venture. We must secure knowledge of their demise or fortune."

"This sounds like a farce. Why deceive me? Don't try to sell fake scat to a manure salesman, General Thynnes."

"I wouldn't dream of it."

"Why would you take the words of a mad-boy so seriously?"

Thynnes reached into his tunic and produced a small roll of parchment. He handed this to Gorias, saying, "I don't know if you can read, but it doesn't matter. I can't read it either, but the oracles swear it's part of the fabled Pnakotic Manuscripts."

Gorias frowned at the parchment.

The General said, "And I need not tell you the implications of such a thing? How would he get his hands on such a manuscript? Only worshipers of the stygian depths would have such a parchment out in a raw country, for this isn't a land of scholars and librarians we go to."

Gorias handed him back the paper and snatched the flask back. Up ending it, he soon said, "There's no good to be had from this place and that damned paper." Mouth transforming into a savage cave, Gorias muttered low, "I thought I destroyed all of these scrolls at Jericho."

"What? You saw something preserved by the Atlantean high-priest Klarkash-Ton?"

"Never you mind...that piece there must be from a copy. You know the stories passed around of the ice monsters and creatures that live on the top of the Earth?"

"They even tell those tales of the Lord of the Pole down where you come from? They say your tribe came from Thule."

"I've been everywhere, General," Gorias snapped, hands digging into his knees. "I hear fairy stories everywhere I go. That's why your damned colony is lost because they didn't heed the old tales. This modern world forgets the stories of the ice ages, of the stories in the Pnakotic Manuscripts of the white flame and his rage."

Thynnes smirked and said, "Aphoom-Zhah. That's the name the kid said."

Gorias frowned and then cursed, for the flask was empty. "Aphoom-Zhah, son of Cthugha, is prisoner in the northlands, set there by the Elder Gods themselves." He wiped his mouth before saying, "Your village is excrement by now."

"Why do you say that?"

"If Aphoom-Zhah is real, then his followers are as well. The Gnoph-keh's were said to be created by Aphoom-Zhah...and they eat people. We better turn back."

Thynnes wore a forlorn look. "There were a few sub human, bestial humanoids that the first settlers hunted for sport. This was near the base of the mountain range called the Eiglophians. I think they called them the Voormi. Some say they cried out to Azathoth and Cxaxukluth to save them."

"Sweet. We are twenty kinds of fucked."

"Bah, pagan scum, all of them."

Gorias' face shuddered. "I'm a man of the Earth, General. I've seen many bad things and monsters best left in the caldron of creation's waste hole. I slew a spawn of a Tsathoggua in the black kingdoms once, conjured by a Sultan's wizard."

Thynnes roared with laughter. "Oh, you jest me now! How did you do that?"

Gorias shrugged, eyes on the ceiling as if he saw the past played out there. "Mastodon stampede, but I digress. We better be stopping for a look see at this land and sailing away, if you are intent on going. There's a reason no civilized or barbarian race lives in these lands."

Thynnes grunted and sat forward. "I've heard the tales of Aphoom-Zhah as well, Gorias. If he was imprisoned by the Outer or Elder Gods as the tales say, and has no form, what did this madman see?"

Gorias shook his head once as if he'd been struck. "Maybe he found a crack in the prison of the Gods." He then sighed. "Did you bring my weapons?"

With a nod, Thynnes confirmed, "Your swords and daggers are here, helmet as well. That's some piece of work, all scooped out from a dragon body."

"Good. I'd hate to meet Wodan unarmed. I've always had this vision of him throwing me off the rainbow bridge for dying stupidly."

As Gorias started to rise up, Thynnes asked him, "Who is Jenna?"

Blue eyes burning at the old General, Gorias seethed, "Where did you hear that name?"

"From you," Thynnes retorted, unafraid. "You said it in the bar and mumble it in your dreams. Was she your lover?"

"My first." Gorias swallowed, eyes looking at the wooden wall, seeing something far away. "She was, and will be again." His voice thickened as he said, "When I near my death, she waits for me. Sometimes, when the rage is on me and the drink is heavy, I can see her." He took a few breaths, stood up into a crouch and said, "But dying in a dungeon is no way to reach her, now is it? I'm a crazy man, getting' old, thinking of the neighbor girl I covered as a lad. That was real though, all nice and sweet. Dunno why she seems so near at times."

Out on the deck again, Thynnes said with a boisterous laugh, "That's the spirit! I like a big man along who has a good reason to die fighting. No telling how much damage you can do."

Gorias let his hair fly in the wind and stared at the distant land and mountains starting to take shape in the noonday's light. He said, "One never knows."

***

While the drakkar pitched forward in the waves, Gorias filled his belly with beef jerky and wine. He listened to Thynnes tell of how they

Author and Finisher of Our Flesh

liberated the sea faring vessels used in the Albion Navy from the Great Race of Thule. Gorias counted forty men rowing and guessed that Thynnes commanded nearly two hundred additional troops on the vessel. By their uniforms, chain mail, leathers, short battle swords and flails, Gorias surmised them as Albion infantry. These weren't green troops, for many of the hard eyed veterans looked Gorias straight in the eye, unimpressed by his legend. The younger regiments of archers and a few axe men were content to ignore the Ingaevone. A few stared, the really green ones, curious over his story. The fellows rowing were naval men, heads shaved, wrapped in towels, and brawnier than the rest. Many of these men looked to be from Thule or other barbarian homelands, as they dwarfed the regular soldiers of Transalpina by quite a margin.

"Wise to steal from the best," said Gorias, waving a hand at the vessel and then the rowers. "These flexible bastards can travel across any sea."

Thynnes gazed overboard, seeing a few dorsal fins emerge through the choppy waters, and said, "They are fast as well, Gorias. I hope to be in and out quick, and back to Albion to carry out my other strategy."

"Maybe that's why the King sent you out here, General, to make sure you die and don't overthrow anyone."

Thynnes eyes bulged and he glared at Gorias. "You...don't think..."

"I don't just fight with my swords. You've been betrayed or the old asswipe on the throne figured you out. Mayeb Silex knows, too. Maybe not, but sometimes even freaky-boys catch a lucky nut."

A grim look spread on Thynnes weathered face as the drakkar loped closer to the edge of the land. "Fah, what if he knows? The military is under my command. They love a warrior more than a freak any day of the month. Most of them are weary of the ravings of an aging miscreant."

Gorias adjusted the strap for his sword across his chest. "You may need my service after all, more than you thought, old prick, if the King is onto your scheming ass. Some of his forces may be loyal to him, or at least his palace guard."

An eyebrow raised at Gorias, Thynnes stated, "He may want to kill everyone on this vessel when we return. You are dogcrap by association then, old Ingaevone."

Gorias roared with laughter, a strange sound to the men, as Gorias had been nothing but despondent since he came into their presence. "That may well be. I'd sooner take my chances back in Albion than with some unnamed horror." Gorias' smile faded as the drakkar moved closer to the docks the colonists had built, stabbing out into the ocean. "My skin is alive with the air of this place. Something is wrong and cold even for this early autumn season."

The beach spread from side to side, somewhat muted with only a short field of sand to trek through. However, they guided the drakkar to the long wooden pier that extended into the ocean. Beyond the beach, Gorias could see tall grasses carry on for several hundred yards before a wider area cleared out. Unable to tell if crops or gardens inhabited this region deforested from the wilderness, Gorias could perceive many homes, barns and cribs beyond.

"The mountains are like a wall behind that community," Thynnes remarked, causing many soldiers to nod in agreement.

"They drape in too close, like a shroud," Gorias declared, thumbs fiddling with the top of his belt. "I see no people coming to greet us, or even signs of the ships that came before from Albion."

Thynnes balled his hands into fists, but they swung at his sides. "Good point. Could they have been lost before they got here?"

Near by the railing, Gorias pointed to the beach and said, "Look far up near where the greenery begins. See? The tide has carried in planks from the water. Those are what remain of your drakkars or karrs, good men of Albion."

A thick armed rower with a bushy beard, shouted, "Piss on you, Ingaevone! I am a Pryten slave!"

Gorias shrugged. "Something tells me that whatever lurks here in this community doesn't give a damn about any of that."

One of the soldiers gave Thynnes a panicked look and said stoutly, "Sir, we should turn back."

"Because of a few broken bits of wood?" Thynnes raged and nearly struck the man. "Not on your life." His gaze returned to the line of brooding hills beyond the village. "We must see what ails this land and our kindred."

The concern shown clear to the soldier's faces and Gorias

shook his head from side to side. When they neared the dock, Gorias hopped up to the railing and said, "If you all would feel better, manly men of Transalpina, I shall go first and walk toward this village. If you can find your balls, follow me."

Gorias leapt off the drakkar and onto the long pier before they properly moored the vessel. His boots tested the logs before he moved farther though and found the walk sturdy. Gorias scanned the land beyond the tall grasses.

"I can see some movement over there, a man moving beyond the village." His words fell flat, as if bored by the sight. "Disembark and let us all..." His deep voice trailed off and Gorias' eyes changed direction, toward the beach. Blinking, Gorias' eyes then widened and his mouth fell open. "Jenna..." he murmured.

The soldiers stood and started to take up their arms or adjust their armor, Thynnes stepped over and stood near Gorias to ask, "What is it? Why do you speak of this Jenna again? This is a bad time to become horny."

Gorias raised his right arm to point at the beach, and then let his hand drop. "My mind tricks me, General. I..."

"Did you see her?" Thynnes inquired, his words low and soft, understanding the Ingaevone at last.

With a quick nod, Gorias let his chin drop, but his eyes still searched the beach. "Yes, she was there, riding her horse. The sunlight makes the red in her mousy brown hair dance."

Thynnes jeered him, saying, "That's pretty poetic for a drunken

Author and Finisher of Our Flesh

Lord."

Anger seized Gorias' face as a few of the soldiers took up what Thynnes was saying. One jabbed at Gorias, saying, "You're very sweet for a Ingaevone, old boy!"

Another fighter glanced down the beach and asked, "Where did you lose this Jenna?"

Fury burned in his hairy face, but Gorias looked away from them, to the sprawling beach and then toward the settlement. "I never lost her." His big hand gently touched his chest, near his heart as he said, "I know exactly where she is."

Gorias walked down the dock and stopped where the ground met the wooden planks. The others started to jump from the drakkar, walking until they noted Gorias stood motionless.

From the waters on either side of the dock came forth dozens of ivory colored shapes. They burst from the waters, ready to strike. Guttural roars in their mouths, these feral beasts swung long, hairy arms at the men of Albion and stabbed long claws at them.

Sword out, Thynnes yelled, "Crap! Voormi!"

Without hesitation, the veterans of Transalpina took the fight to the fabled man-beasts of the hills, come down to attack intruders to their realm.

A few of the fighters were taken by surprise, their legs ripped open and bodies hauled from the docks and into the icy water. The other soldiers of General Thynnes proved their mettle in a moment's time. Steel slid from scabbards and the men shouted cries of battle, either from their own courage, honor to their mothers or their gods. True warrior grit flowed as they stabbed at their enemies, driving the hairy beasts back into the water, in most cases dead or dismembered. Small swords split skulls like melons and brains soon made the dock slippery.

Thynnes himself beheaded one of the Voormi, causing the head to roll to Gorias's boots. The Ingaevone thought the maw of the Voormi hideous, almost like a gorilla of the dark kingdoms, but with ivory hair and a mouth full of gigantic canine teeth.

One of the beasts made it to Gorias on the ground, crawling, for one of the soldiers sliced a muscle loose from the back of its calf. Never drawing a weapon, Gorias kicked the hairy man-beast in the face, making the Voormi to arch its back, putting it in line for Bekan to split its skull with his great axe. Brains colored carroty and gray spilled from either side of the wedged skull, accenting the ivory shoulders of the beast before it fell over.

As suddenly as the contemptible attack started, the creatures receded. The soldiers of Albion waved their weapons and hurled curses at their attackers, daring them to come forth again and get them. A couple pulled out quivers and shot into the waters, daring them to attack anew.

"By the rings of Cykranosh, I think I know where your settlement is," said Gorias, eyes glassy as he gestured toward the mountains and the figure moving amongst the cottages.

About to make more mirth on the hulking Ingaevone, the crew

of the drakkar fell silent as their eyes took in the sight only Gorias comprehended. In only a few moments, the shock spread to the entire crew.

The initial vision showed that this persona strode as a very big man. But on closer inspection, they all beheld that no settler walked in the abandoned place, nor was he just a creature of thuggish proportions. From the distance, it aped a form of a regular man for some time, but it only took a minute for the perspective to change. In reality, the figure loomed above the cottages, dropping heavy steps so hard the footfalls sounded out. Though they didn't echo, every soldier on the dock and rower on the drakkar paused to stare where the sound originated.

"Damn," was all Gorias could say at first.

The giant individual, in the silhouette of a man, faced them and started to step their way. With a stride several yards long, it reached the edge of the village and stood by the overgrown gardens. From there, the sunlight showed over its skin. When the scarlet hued flesh of the creature became clear to the men from the ship, the soldiers turned and started to retreat to the drakkar.

Only Gorias and Thynnes remained at the end of the dock, staring back at the figure that aimed its colossal head toward them.

Thynnes gasped, "Impossible to tell if this thing looks at us for real. It has no eyes, yet there's something in the rounded spots that passes for eye sockets."

Gorias said, "I doubt they could see anything." After all, both could see that the eyeballs were men curled in the fetal position. "The entire damn thing is made of human beings."

From the thudding feet, up its thick legs, to the top of its long head, the figure thrived with humanoid forms. All of them clung to the shape, naked, reddish in hue, and perfectly in sync to make the contour of a man.

It raised its right hand and pointed at them. Its fingers were men, each a man of some substance. No bond or lash fixed them in place, nothing material bound them that either foreigner could discern. Indistinct in their appearance, impossible to tell if they were from Transalpina or mercenary soldiers sent to see what happened to the settlers, they all were a niche in the amalgamation that was this being.

Thynnes started to back up when Bekan unleashed a shrilled scream, "It's the god of the Gnoph-kehs! Let us begone before it's too late."

With a slap to Gorias's back, Thynnes gave a grunt to certify his agreement. "By the gods, Gorias, let us be away from here. It's clear to me now that no amount of men before could best that thing."

Gorias started to back up. Though he thought an army of his Ingaevone brethren may give it a shot, his natural fear told him that this creature added to itself somehow. Every hair on his flesh writhed as if drawn to the giant.

As he retreated, never turning his back on the approaching

wonder, he heard a voice he first thought to be Thynnes or one of the crew. When the giant stopped and leered at Gorias, scant yards from the tall grasses near the beach, he understood where the voice originated.

"In a world of the ordinary, come unto us, you who are extraordinary," The smooth, calm tone spoke in Gorias' head. "You are unlike them and should not be among those gnats. Come unto us, great warrior of the ages. Come be one with us and add your voice to the choir that is Aphoom-Zhah."

Tremors of ice trickled down his muscled arms as Gorias continued to back away from the giant claiming to be the polar god of renown.

The voice spoke to Gorias again. "See all that we are and what you can be, little one. Be with us, be us and look down on all of humanity. You can be overlord of them and those who dwell in the bowels of Voormithadreth."

A chorus of voices agreed with the first, then encouraged Gorias to join them.

Gorias shook his head, then turned and brought up the rear of the men piling back onto the drakkar. Already, the sailors had cast off lines, ready to push off. Gorias stood on the dock and looked down at the edge of the boat. Bekan almost reached out to him to pull him aboard, but the icy blue eyes of the Ingaevone drilled into him. Though armed with a twin headed steel axe, Bekan knew better than to lay hands on Gorias.

Thynnes said with nervous strength, "Whatever horror that is, truly, 'Twas the fate of the settlers and the parties. Come, let us not add to its...appetite."

Just as Gorias lifted his boot, he looked down the beach again. The image of Jenna on her horse staring at him set his heart to thudding more than the monster near to the sands. Her blue eyes practically gave him an accusing look. They looked from Gorias, to the boat and then to Gorias again.

Her voice, gentle and true to her manner, said to him, "You cannot reach me that way, Gorias." She then stared back at the monster.

"Jenna calls me," Gorias said and snatched the double headed axe from Bekan's hands. The young soldier shouted, but never went after his weapon.

Gorias squared his shoulders to the creature beyond the sands, passing the axe to his left hand and unsheathed a sword on his back with his right.

Thynnes grabbed the edge of the boat and shouted, "The creature deceives you, Gorias! I can hear it in my head as well. Run and get on this ship before it is too late!"

Gorias stared at Jenna, Her face was softer, and now her voice full of tears as she whispered, "Come to me, Gorias."

When Gorias started to run forward, the soldiers howled a shout of angst, then a roar of excitement at the warrior's bravado. Surely, he rushed to his death, but they saluted his strength, no matter how mad.

Gorias heard Thynnes say something about bringing out long bows, but all he could see was the looming humanoid shape in front of him. Though educated by life, a Ingaevone lived on instinct. Gorias felt uneasy that a god created this creature. He wasn't so certain an entity that fancied himself a deity didn't do it, though. Natural instincts told him to flee.

"This thing must die," he whispered.

Gorias understood he could never reach Jenna in the realms beyond death by running away. However, if he could try to kill this Aphoom-Zhah, and this thing slew him, they would be together before evening.

Though the creature stood on the sands, the marvel before Gorias started to wear on the Ingaevone. The thing even had genitals, he mused to himself, gripping his weapons. Why did it make two men curl into the shape of testicles while two more swung free between its legs? Gorias thought, because whatever made this recalled having them.

Running forward, calling on the name of Wodan, Gorias threw the axe, end over end, toward the giant's balls. If the thing possessed a groin structure, the axe buried itself in its upper thigh, near to this spot. The giant calling itself Aphoom-Zhah steadied itself, but never fell. Gorias ran forward and jumped at the right calf of the entity, inserting his sword's blade deep into the supple flesh.

Gorias discovered that the soft tissue constructed of humanoid figures too elastic for his boots sank into the top of its foot. Though he experienced no trouble cutting a section of calf loose, he then saw the figures move toward him. As he turned to retreat, arms fell on him and Gorias felt pulled up into the flesh of Aphoom-Zhah.

A sensation like drowning in thick, bubbly water ran over Gorias. Though he'd drawn in air, he didn't seem to want to breathe any longer. It was as if he felt the entire outline of the creature, and his mind grew afire, even if his limbs felt very cold. A slicker of liquid ran over his body and Gorias started to lose where he was in the mass of bodies.

A hundred of voices assailed his mind, some screaming, some weeping, but they all seemed to meld into one voice as the seconds went by. As his skin felt colder, Gorias picked up on thoughts, of the purpose for this monstrosity...that Aphoom-Zhah really resided far away...and had added strength to this being to free himself.

Yes, Aphoom-Zhah indeed dwelt a prison far north, below the sea, and he created this creature to liberate him from his torment. Gorias sensed the thing as incomplete, but wondered if his escape would soon be impossible. So comfortable and soothing he found his place of residence in the beast, he didn't want to try and fight it any longer. It warmed him like a drunken stupor and the embrace of a million whores.

Author and Finisher of Our Flesh

Though his own eyes grew blind, Gorias could see in his mind...or through the eyes of the beast, the lands around him... them. From out of the base of the mountain, not seen from the sea, clusters of the Voormi congregated, worshiping the creature form of Aphoom-Zhah. Several furry beasts with six legs started to emerge from tunnels in the mountain. Unsure of what they were, perhaps the Gnoph-kehs, Gorias then saw the village, empty of human life, much of it scattered to pieces and in a state of decay.

All the while, he heard the relaxing voices around him, different, yet uttering similar words. They wanted him as one of them, part of this bizarre collective. They didn't want him to be one of the barbarians, or even the gallant knights of Transalpina, but one of them, exactly like them, doing and saying exactly what they did. Suddenly, Gorias comprehended the terror that was Aphoom-Zhah, and at its simplest, he couldn't swim in this flesh or be apart of their deluded fantasy realm any longer. Sensing his plan to rebel, they told him he may die if he stepped outside of the accepted collective, forever to walk as an outcast. Together, they had a sense of self, a fantastic ideal Gorias saw as a delusion of grandness.

Gorias felt it would be better to die as himself than live amongst them...better death than a piece of the crowd. In fact, as his hatred of the feelings they sent him grew, he focused and the rage in his mind burned. The icy feelings of his skin faded and he felt his toes, fingers and own flesh...steel still in his grip.

His forearms twisted and rent the flesh about him open. The dew nails of the dragon on his forearms cut him a path. It took all of his strength, but after the sensation of oneness faded, Gorias flailed and pushed through the mass of tightening flesh. His fingers broke into the air and the forms around him lurched. His sword pushed out, creating a larger space, but the weapon slipped from his wet grasp. His bleary eyes saw that he was much higher in the creature than he first thought, about mid thigh on the right side. Trying to pull himself loose, yet not wanting to plummet headfirst to the beach, Gorias fought with the gaggle of hands and arms, trying to pull him back into the being.

Once outside the flesh a little, he saw that the creature peppered with shafts from longbows. Had his own strength extracted himself from this collective, or had the archers in the drakkar aided? It didn't matter, for Gorias could breathe again.

Unable to free his left arm, Gorias pulled hard still and yanked free the curled up figure of an elderly female. Eyes shut, she screamed out in a liquidy call, trying to scratch and claw Gorias back into the fold. Try as she might, the old woman couldn't get a handle on Gorias. She screamed and told him so many things, grand tales of why he should stay with the collective. No longer willing to listen to her pathetic lies, Gorias acted. Her tongue kept wagging as he seized her. All twisted and rosy colored, Gorias tossed her free of the collective and sent her screaming to the beach. Her brittle back busted and the pitiful screams from her gaping mouth ceased at last.

Like he spotted the gate to heaven itself, Gorias saw the handle of the axe near the groin of the giant. He ripped the weapon loose and roared the name of his god once more. Fingers, hands and mouths slaked over his frame, but Gorias fought on. No longer could he hear Jenna's voice, or that of the collective, but the tone of his father came back to him. It sounded like a berserk scream.

Caught in the morass, he kicked, feeling tendons tear and bones crunch. He wedged his body and the hand that gripped the weapon came loose. With a single arm, he swung the great axe, Wodan came through and Gorias sank it into the lower abdomen of the creature. Negative cries filled his mind, like a gasp of a choir in a well. He still could hear the pleas of the collective to join them. Gorias twisted the axe sideways, then pulled back. Though no guts unraveled, a pair of arms and an entire body puked from the belly of the thing that personified Aphoom-Zhah. Gorias couldn't tell if the cry came from within his mind or actually to his ears, but he heard a wail of agony.

Legs shaky in the wet flesh of the giant, but ready to propel him away, Gorias jumped free of the creature and plummeted downward. He guessed the fall at over a dozen feet, but his boots hit the sand, which gave some, and he rolled on the soft earth. Though pain shot up his legs and back, it felt good to be alive. It was good to be just Gorias again. Beside where he landed, he saw his sword. Gorias smiled.

He turned to face his opponent and saw the immense being wobble. From the injury to the leg and the shot to its gut, the collective stumbled, but held its ground. Gorias seized the axe with both hands, reached back far behind his head and flung it, end over end. This time, he still missed the head, but the axe tore into the neck of the beast. The blow caused a waterfall of grisly ejecta down the chest of the monster. This substance held many bodies and more wriggling lives. The neck weakened, the large oblong head of Aphoom-Zhah teetered and hung over on its ruined root.

From out of the brush emerged one of the Gnoph-kehs, loping on its six legs, opening its huge mouth to roar at Gorias as Aphoom-Zhah came apart. Gorias thought the new arrival a freakish polar bear, but far bigger. Mind still confused, arms sore, but ablaze with fire, Gorias brought out his other sword and swung both blades as he dodged the attack of the massive creature. Any other animal, his falling slash would've taken off a limb, but his swords lodged deep in the thigh of the Gnoph-keh's left fore-leg. When the Gnoph-keh lurched, shocked by the impediment to its advance, Gorias' body jerked, not letting go of his weapon. He wrenched them back, pulled free and stabbed forth, delving the tip into the side of the beast a foot deep at least. The creature yelped and drew away from him, making the blades exit at a crude angle, bringing a loop of intestine with it.

Gorias turned and ran for the drakkar. His legs rebelled at first, but after a few steps, they got with the program. The ship sloshed out in the sea several yards. Thynnes and the men shouted their support as Gorias swam for them. He never looked back, but the horror in the faces of the men on the ship told him a story.

As soon as several men dragged Gorias aboard, he learned the reason for their terror. More of the six-legged polar bear-like beasts flooded around the giant as it fell to pieces. Many headed to the beach, aimed at the ocean, but a few stopped, looked at the flesh disgorging all over the sand, and started to dine. The creatures tore into the pile of unraveling humanity while a few of their brethren swam toward the drakkar.

The sailors tossed javelins, impaling a few of them as the long bowmen fired a fresh volley.

The ship turned and started to head into open water. Gorias stared at the beach for a long time before he muttered, "She's gone."

"You'll see her again, Gorias," Thynnes said gently, his own eyes still on the distant land. "Just not today."

Gorias sat in the rear of the boat and breathed heavily. One of the sailors brought him a ragged cloth rag to wipe off his skin. He rubbed his eyes, then held his face in his hands as Thynnes stood near him. The sailor dropped the towel and stepped away from Gorias.

The Ingaevone asked the General, "Do you believe in God?"

Thynnes shrugged as he peered back at the land again. "A host of them, heh. I reckon there's one that reigns supreme."

"I'm not asking for Valhalla, nor a bevy of drink and whores, hell, I don't even want to piss in the mouth of Cthulhu. All I want is her back. I'd give my left arm to just have a drink with her again." He looked up and let out a tired laugh. He grabbed up the towel, sponged at his face and then wiped down his arms. "And you still want me to kill the pervert King Silex of Albion?"

Thynnes smiled and the ship heaved on, departing with great speed. "Life goes on, Gorias. No use wallowing in loss forever."

Though anger ran through Gorias' brow, he nodded at Thynnes. The harsh words rang true, even if he didn't want to hear them.

"What else can you offer me, but my life and some recompense? My ass grows tired of war, old man."

Thynnes clucked at the sky and then said, "My sister's betrothed died in battle before she consummated the marriage. She is almost twenty winters and of royal blood..."

A doubtful look later, Gorias asked, "A twenty year old virgin? That can't be true or very healthy."

"Does it matter if she is a virgin?"

His hands rung out the rag as he watched the salt water and slime splatter on the boards. Gorias shrugged. "Why would I want her or why would she want me? What do you mean by all of this crazy talk?"

Thynnes smiled. "If you kill Silex and marry her, my, that would add to you legitimacy."

"To what?" Gorias frowned as he wiped his beard off, confused by his words.

"Kingship."

Gorias blinked and stood abruptly. His sinewy arms braced the railing near the rear of the drakkar. He stared toward Albion, though he couldn't see it. He swallowed hard, he licked his mustache, tasting the salt of the sea and the bile of Aphoom-Zhah.

"King," he murmured. "I'd be a real prize for that land, a warrior King."

Thynnes smirked and whispered, "All hail Gorias, King of the Bastards, aye?"

"King of the Bastards, that'd be me," Gorias said and touched his chest near his heart. "How long ago did this girl's lover die in battle?"

"Not really her lover, more of a betrothed, arranged kind of thing. Him? Oh, he was killed by some bastard barbarian in a tavern a fortnight ago."

THE END?

Insurmountable

Insurmountable

*"The superior man is unassuming in his speech,
but exceeds in his actions."*
-CONFUCIUS

The hole in the roof of the shrine didn't gape wide enough to free his father's spirit, so Gorias tossed another dead dwarf over the cliff. The impact of the projectile on the already broken thatched roof proved one Gorias La Gaul desired. Gorias' brow furrowed when the edges of the ragged opening to the monastery broke open further. He rubbed his gray beard and contemplated his next move. With a sigh, Gorias reached down to the snowy earth and grabbed another of the diminutive, albino folk. After he concentrated to make his throw exact, Gorias flung the body, past the stabbing pines and again, hit the target. The body passed through the opening, clipping the ruined thatch so it busted once more.

"Damn," Gorias cursed, hands to the knee plates of this

dragon-skin armor. "I should've gouged open the roof more from the church rafters. Ya'd think in five hundred years I'd be bright enough to know that. Still, I need the blood of the dwarves for the sacrifice."

Determined to kill two projects at once, he armed up another dwarf's body and then looked over at the larger form in the snow, stained crimson. Gorias frowned, staring into the face of his father.

Ambiorix, the Ingaevone, stared back at his son. Then again, Ambiorix would look at anyone, forever. The aging chieftain, frozen solid years ago, sat as stiff as a statue and retained a similar stony hue. Still clutching a battle-axe with both hands, Ambiorix's eyes remained open and his alabaster skin took on an ethereal appearance.

Gorias threw the slain dwarf over the edge and said to his sire, "I can see why these little pricks worshiped you, Father, dumb bastards that they are." The brood of small ones took it hard when Gorias arrived to take their god away.

Though the cold air that came off Zenghaus Mountain bit into the strapping Ingaevone, Gorias never hurried in his task. His cloak and light armor kept him plenty warm. The blood shed on the snow by these tiny folk had long since congealed and the quick battle with them hardly worth recalling.

"The sooner I send enough of you through the roof below," said Gorias to the bodies, then his voice trailed off. He looked up at the sky and contemplated; *the sooner I'll have to drag his corpse down to the shrine.* He still found himself putting off a mission that eluded him for years.

Gorias tried to banish wistful thoughts. However, he soon started chewing over the years that passed since his father sat on one of the peaks of Zenghaus above the terminus line, and promptly froze to death. Too much emotion was bad, Ambiorix taught his village back in Thule. Gorias understood that idea as truth from experiencing life. Though not well read, the Ingaevone chief proved correct. If Gorias let his anger, greed or lust get the better of him, he ended up with his balls in a vice, or sometimes in the clutches of a dolt with no sense of humor. He tried not to focus on silly things. If he really were that gullible, Gorias reasoned, he'd believe the silly stories about the world's immanent destruction in a flood.

A distant groan interrupted his thoughts. Gorias peered up the slope toward the tree line where the sound originated. Without concern, he grabbed another body for an additional volley. However, Gorias jerked from his thoughts as the carcass screamed once he flung it. Flailing in the air, the dwarf who played possum on the snow bank screeched all the way down, but went silent as his body hit the roof, crashed through and bounced inside the provisional temple. Gorias started to laugh as he heard the dwarf bawl again.

"What a survivor, the damned runt." Gorias chuckled at the irony of the dwarf's endurance skills and gave a mock salute. "His back must be broken by now. I'll strangle him in time, aye Father?"

Gorias looked down at the sanctuary and counted on his fingers the number of bodies he'd dispatched. He nodded, wagering that the gap would be wide enough. A smirk spread on his bearded face, for aside from the wail of the paralyzed dwarf, Gorias could hear the plaintive mewlings from around the temple ebbing away. Though he didn't relish the chore at hand, one he'd put off for eons, he found himself amused by weak people, as always.

He stepped near to his swords, both sticking out of the snow. Once he'd pulled a cloth from his belt pouch, he wiped each blade before replacing it in the scabbards on his back. As he did so, he recalled the voices of those down at the monastery, the brides of God himself.

"Our god, Kangmi, will destroy you," the women of the log monastery had spat at Gorias when he dismounted his stallion, Traveler, earlier in the day. "How dare you come unto the sacred mountain, unto the brides of the Man of the Snows, on a fool's errand?"

The half dozen female supplicants of the temple all stood great with child. Their samite gowns bulged in testimony of this fact and from their words, the fruits of the mountain spirit.

"I just stopped here to warm up and feed my horse before I retrieve my father," Gorias told them. "Word from a friend told me his body slid down from the place where he died. I know he travels around the summits of there. You folks don't concern me."

Insurmountable

The dark haired woman in charge had cursed Gorias like a dried out whore, and then told him, "The false god of the snows who holds the axe? The Stipnca's worship him, foolish children who find his roving image god-like. What do they know of gods? They who were created by--"

Gorias shot back, "I don't care who made them. The fact that my father's body moves around this damned elevation after his death is nothing but a jest of the gods. If you knew anything of gods, you'd know what a petty lot of pricks they can be. They made him go down lower on the crest to force me to my obligation."

Snide voices of the women rang out at once, all saying to Gorias, "Kangmi will slay you and use your manhood as a bottle for his newborns."

Gorias blinked, trying to forget the women and their words... or their screams as he crucified them to the doors of the temple. Not that either event bothered him, really, he tried to focus on the task. Like he did earlier, Gorias pushed the frozen figure down the mountain. Soon, he'd retrieve his horse to do more of the work. Ambiorix then slipped from his grip and thudded to the snows, surrounded in a corona of Stipnca blood.

"Your worshipers provided a final sacrifice, Father," Gorias jeered his dead forbearer. "The tiny whoresons probably loved dying for you. Rotten tit-mice, every one of them." His mane of long hair blew free in the wind and he added, "Their blood will entreat Wodan in the end, so they get to provide twice."

From down off the mountain, a rumble rolled that he at first mistook for thunder. Gorias wasn't foolish enough to discount what his senses told him. Setting his boots on either side of his father, Gorias' nose enlightened him that something foul approached. His ears recorded the crunch of the snow not far off. Gorias spotted the deep prints he assumed belonged to the Kangmi when first encountering the tiny Stipncas on the mountain. He quickly dispensed his heavy woolen cover to allow his arms freer movement, then reached behind his head and grabbed the pommels of his twin swords.

Over the snowdrifts leapt Kangmi in all his transcendent glory. When Kangmi landed a few yards from him, towering over the thuggish Ingaevone, Gorias wondered what the children squirming in those women's bellies would look like. As he drew out the swords from his back, Gorias ruminated that the world would never know.

Though Kangmi's overall body frame bore a humanoid shape, his outline shared kinship with jungle beasts Gorias once beheld in his journeys south of Kemet and west of Zimbabwe. Kangmi's stance, not unlike that of an upside down horseshoe, spewed long arms from his shoulders until they touched the snows. His hands, big enough to cradle a man's skull, sported fingernails that raked long patterns in the snow. Heavy white fur covered Kangmi's body, but his chest and abdomen exhibited a bluish colored skin, somewhat hidden by long wisps of ivory hair. Enormous feet kept the creature in place and his incredible manhood swung down practically to his knees. A mouth full of canine teeth parted to let a howl escape.

But Kangmi's chest rose and fell. He breathed; thus, even an illiterate barbarian could understand that Kangmi can die. Gorias La Gaul, centuries from his life as a Lord, was no barbarian.

Pinkish eyes with black pupils leered first at Gorias, then the blades gleaming in the daylight, and settled at last on the few leftover bodies of the Stipncas. Flabby lips peeled back and fetid breath carried the words, "You've slain my children."

Though in a defensive pose over his father's body, Gorias blinked. Was this a bluff to throw him off guard? Gorias comprehended the power of misdirection and had used it himself to distract dense opponents. One might exclaim that the floor ran alive with snakes, even though one's enemies had just trod on it. Chances were, for a split second, the adversary would look down or away from you. Ambiorix instructed Gorias long ago that a second was all one needed and death was easy to deal to the stupid.

Gorias swallowed, sized up at the god standing before him, then thought of the deity lying frozen between his legs and reflected, *so was religion*.

He wasn't about to argue with Kangmi. After all, Kangmi was a beast. Ambiorix educated Gorias that one tames, hunts, kills, skins, and usually, eats beasts. When Kangmi's mouth tightened, Gorias comprehended the creature planned to swing a claw.

Knowing a headshot or blow to the heart from his sword would be impossible to land on the creature, Gorias leaned forward and dove. The massive hands started to swing down toward him.

Gorias' swords twirled, and he stabbed downward as if wielding a spear, using the beast's enormous feet to its disadvantage.

Some sing ballads over the swords of Gorias La Gaul that they are made from angel's wings...others say that they were made from a smithy in Shynar, a huge sonofabitch and the major whore-taker of a village, but either way his ability with metals couldn't be denied. Whatever their origin, the weapon never broke as Gorias dropped all of his weight behind the blows, stabbing the swords through the tops of Kangmi's feet. When Gorias' momentum carried him ass over elbows, the blades stayed in place, refusing to leave the bones of the gigantic feet or the frigid earth underneath them.

The howls of the inhuman fiend reminded Gorias of when he'd heard a mastodon fall into a lava flow near Engaruka.

Long arms in the air, Kangmi screamed on and tried to turn, thus twisting the swords in his feet even more. Blood spurted from the wounds, painting his pallid calves with jets of crimson. A stream of this blood lapped over the chest of the prone Ambiorix. He'd had blood on him before, Gorias mused, and the old chief took it in stride.

Even if Gorias charged and sent Kangmi over the cliff down

the slope, he reckoned a brute from this terrain would survive that fall. The blades contained his only salvation, but reaching for them meant death, especially since Kangmi had started to lean down and gripped the pommels. Gorias counted his options. The daggers in his belt could only work at close range. He ran his left hand over the dew nail on his right fore-arm bracket, a piece of bone from the dragon's leg skinned for his armor.

Gorias did what all survivors do. He reached down for a weapon, and found the stiffened ankles of one of the Stipncas he'd slain earlier. Gorias set his boots in the snow and swung the body like a bludgeon. The dead dwarf connected with the slumped over skull of Kangmi. So intent was the monster in removing the weapons from his feet, the beast didn't dodge the blow. The skull of the Stipnca broke open on Kangmi like a rotten melon. Be it from extreme cold, a lack of dexterity or brains, the Stipnca's head splattered, spewing orange and gray slop over the giant's face. As the swords fell free, Kangmi staggered, wiping the grime from his visage. Through the muck, Gorias saw the body had succeeded in busting Kangmi's lips open on the row of brutal teeth.

When Gorias pulled dual daggers out of his waist belt, he stepped forward. Kangmi gaped down at him, still in pain, but half amused by the stranger's pluck.

"You're mad, human," Kangmi coughed, rage bubbling, dropping his arms down.

Gorias hadn't the speed to block the blows this time, and felt each hand chop, one on the shoulder, and the other on the side of his head. Gorias flipped over, head full of stars, crumpling to the snow. If his shoulder dislocated he felt a wicked pain as it popped back in upon his landing.

Certain the moment of his death drew nigh, Gorias struggled to banish the drunken feeling in his brain and flipped over in the snow to escape an additional attack. When he did, a set of balled up hairy fists smashed into the icy ground, just missing him.

Gorias lay back, feigning inertia. The ruse lasted long enough for Kangmi to stagger a few steps, raise both arms high and give a death yell any Ingaevone would've been jealous to make.

The beast didn't call on Wodan, but Gorias did. His death-shriek joined that of Kangmi when he dove, avoiding the massive arms, but setting himself just in the spot he desired: Between the creature's legs, Gorias raised the daggers, burying one on either side of Kangmi's large testicles. The creature convulsed, and then seemed frozen for a moment as Gorias performed a maneuver usually meant to slice the throat of a man in two places from behind. This time, a gelding was needed and the sack fell free easier than Gorias would've thought. A wellspring of blood and veins erupted out like a burst barrel of beer on Equinox Night.

Though his voice shrilled to a higher pitch, and agony surely seized his flesh, Kangmi reached down and grabbed Gorias by the hair. Just before the trembling Kangmi yanked Gorias away, the Ingaevone dropped a knife and thrust his right forearm toward the gaping wound. The dew nail of the dragon armor probed the hole, reaching for anything solid. When the beast pulled on him, Gorias yanked veins and a loop of something he couldn't name out of the beast.

Such was his anguish; Kangmi let Gorias drop from his grip and stepped backwards.

Free of the shadow of the colossal creature, Gorias scooped up his swords. Measuring the vacillating god of the mountain, he swung his blades with great force. Kangmi's left hand came up to block the shot, as his right hand engrossed his ruined groin.

Gorias' slashing left sword shot took off four fingers, causing Kangmi additional hurt, bringing tears from the monster's eyes. Gorias didn't fault him that.

Eyes darting, Gorias surveyed behind Kangmi--reading the battlefield as he always did--and attacked. Aggressively criss-crossing his swipes, he drove Kangmi back, not once connecting with him, but making him go where he wanted. Gorias then charged, slamming his right shoulder into Kangmi's stomach. The blow merely knocked the wavering beast off balance, but the gory foot injury made the creature slip in the snow. When he fell, he crashed, flopping over the stationary body of Ambiorix, giving out a surprised bray, and then fell silent.

Gorias leapt on the beast's pelvis and held the swords high. Screaming the name of his god, Gorias drove the blades into Kangmi's heart. Though a thick resistance met his thrusts, Gorias overcame the muscle and bones, quickly finding his way to the heart. The creature convulsed and gagged as Gorias twisted the swords around, making sure he destroyed its life center.

Kangmi turned, knocking Gorias off himself, and rolled over. Though Gorias landed cock-eyed in the snow, skating to his knees, he rose up fast, and happy the beast had performed the move. It saved him the trouble of rolling the brute off his father.

Ambiorix's battle-axe stuck out of Kangmi's spine. The fist and forearm of Ambiorix also were present, busted off in the action. Gorias sucked wind as Kangmi breathed his last.

"Damn, you're still a killer, you old sinner," Gorias murmured, smiling at his father's body.

Gorias pulled the piece from the back of Kangmi and laid it on his father's chest. He then started to wipe off the swords on the Kangmi's furry leg. He contemplated what Kangmi said, that the little ones here were his children. Was this so? Gorias pondered the dwarves, how their hair and flesh shone similar to the beast, but, then again, they were half human. Probably not the results the creature wanted with his brides down the mountain, Gorias guessed, but one looks after one's children no matter what.

After he sheathed the swords, Gorias retrieved his cloak. The Stipncas had worshiped Ambiorix, even though their own patron was venerated as a deity by these deluded women down the hillside. Gorias wondered, did they--like most children--seek a different way, or were they just that ignorant?

Insurmountable

Leaving that mystery for the ether, Gorias picked up his father's legs and started to haul him down the mountain. Though too much sentiment wasn't good, Gorias felt a great penance lay in wait for him for avoiding his duty to Ambiorix. Oh, Wodan was an uncaring god and Gorias never prayed to him, save to venerate his name in war or at the climax of a sexual act.

Wodan's son, Donar, though, attempted to do good by him. Donar Tanarus drank, fought, and fornicated in his great hall with all those warriors of his kindred. There it was that Ambiorix sat, on the doorstep of heavenly Tir Na Nog, frozen all these years, caught in time.

Gorias was busy, fighting, seeking wealth, killing, running, becoming a Lord, whoring … and now felt something wayfaring warriors seldom felt. Guilt. He wished to sit at the table of Donar with his father someday, to partake in the eternal feast and the following fornications. Now, he had to do more than just burn the body of his father.

When he saw the monastery of Kangmi and his weeping brides nailed to the outside of it, Gorias discerned that Wodan provided a route for his salvation.

It took a few days for Gorias to thaw his father by the fireplaces inside the temple. Gorias never considered that when he hatched his plan to begin with. The change of plans had made him take down the crucified brides of Kangmi, and even let them tend their wounds.

He slept in a side prayer room, filling his belly on the bread and wine meant for communion with Kangmi from afar. He hoped the elixir of communion wasn't made from Kangmi's own seed, as some religions did to honor a false god. Subsequent to filling his guts, he didn't really care.

On the third day, satisfied his father would burn, Gorias started to build an altar in the main hall of the small temple. Over the stiffening bodies of a dozen dwarves, he stacked as much of the chopped wood that the ladies of Kangmi kept in storage. He saturated this pile with as much oil for lanterns as he could find. Atop this, he placed the body of his father and looked up. Surely, the spirit of his father could escape through that hole.

Before he struck the fire to send his father away forever, Gorias nailed the women up to the outside of the temple again.

As they cursed him, Gorias told them, "Be kind, ladies. I never raped you. You will go to serve my father, who'll be in heaven soon. I had to let you live a few days longer. You'd have escaped to your own afterlife, not to mine. Take care and stop crying, or he'll throw you over the rainbow bridge to the Satyrs who only desire buggery in eternal burning Ifurin."

Gorias then struck the flints and set the oil supplies to burn. Fire crept through the structure and over the pile of wood. The Ingaevone warrior climbed into the saddle on Traveler and watched the fires lick the temple, creeping out all over.

He once heard a sage say that one's father should be as a god to you. Gorias figured this to be manure, but he hoped his actions succeeded in honoring his father enough in the end. Gorias saw the ashes arise toward the heavens and he turned to go, noting the screams of the women, yet, thinking how much they'd soon be singing at the great hall of the dead in the eternal land of youth, in service to Ambiorix.

He didn't know if he'd ever be the man his father was, or if he'd produce offspring to compliment him so. That task proved great indeed. But that labor wasn't for the hands of men to fret over. God would provide for the strong weapons to wage a life and provide respect in death.

He always did.

THE END

Beginning of the Trail

Beginning of the Trail

"A desperate disease requires a dangerous remedy."
-GUY FAWKES, 1605

My, what a man you are, drawing out the two legendary swords made from angel's wings to slay a simple priest. Is it true that fabled hero Gorias La Gaul has no heart?"

"I'm about as much a hero as you are a priest."

Two gleaming short swords drove through the man clad in a long robe pinning him up against the trunk of the birch tree.

"Let me up to the ceremony site or I'll kill all of you."

The man with two swords through his chest didn't answer. Gorias didn't expect one from him. He hoped sticking the mouthy leader of the group blocking the road to a tree would inspire compliance with the others. Even impaled twice below his short ribs, Gorias thought his target owned the expression of a jackass.

It took a cocky bastard to step out into the dirt road from the copse to hold up ten soldiers in the regalia of the Transalpinan army and not to mention two hard cases clad in armor.

The sound of swords clearing scabbards rang out and a voice behind him yelled, "Baal's balls, Gorias! He's just a priest." The largest of the military men on horseback, a bear of a man near to Gorias' size, cursed his soldiers who held out blades as he drew a short sword secured to his thick waist belt. "Cyrus, Nahum! To my side! Yavin? Where the hell is Yavin?"

A half dozen men who'd melted into the roadway from the forest brandished curved swords. Even though dressed in russet colored robes only a Cleric would don, the swords testified to the truth of Gorias' next statement: "He ain't no priest, General Thynnes." Fists tight on the pommels, Gorias twisted his blades, causing the man's eyes to widen and arms to flail at his shoulders, pulling Gorias' faded over cloak off partially. The six men from the woods didn't come to aide their brother, but stayed in the road leading up to the hill ahead, where cries of anger and the clanging of weapons echoed.

The men on horseback behind Gorias started to dismount. Ten of them wore leathers, chain mail, and sported military insignias. The other man, bald, thick set, wore heavier armor and leggings, but didn't dismount. They couldn't stop the armed priests that hemmed the road in close from attacking Gorias. Two of the robed men jabbed at the warrior, breaking their bronze blades on Gorias' bluish armor.

Gorias' long white hair swooped back as he pulled his swords from the dying man, letting the body go to its knees and fall into his thighs. Moving one leg back and squaring his shoulders to his attackers, Gorias swiped out with his twin blades. He removed the wrist of the nearest man, who still gaped at his broken sword as his appendage flew off. Gorias left him to ponder the blood gouting from his stump and sliced the man on his opposite side open from the wrist to the elbow, making sure he'd never wield a sword, much less hold his manhood to pee again.

"This is bad," a stout man amongst Thynnes' military troopers swore as he stayed in the saddle, looking to the sacrosanct site above, not concerned about the battle in front of him, hand resting on his long mustache striped gray like a badger pelt.

Gorias looked across the tall grasses and up the hill at the religious site. The locale, Woodsborough, sat high on the flat-topped knoll, it's monoliths made of huge logs that aped great stone circles in Albion across the channel. Through the ruckus of Thynnes' troopers dismembering the fake priest honor guard, Gorias could hear trouble up on the hillock.

"The Queen's party is in sorry shape, maybe dead already up there by now," Gorias stated and swore, swiping his swords through the man's robe which fell off his thighs, exposing his under tunic and bare skin. He pointed with his right blade. "See? Damned Pryten markings, tattoos and woad colorings under their costumes."

Thynnes kicked the dying man in the head and did a double take as one of his men, a fair-haired youth named Cyrus, struggled with one of the robed figures who wrapped a whip about his sword arm. "Pryten savages or pirates, damn them. They have no place here. Queen Garnet and the royal family are up there with their party of aristocrats and hangers-on."

Gorias joined his gaze on the hill and they saw a body in purple clothing stumble to the edge of the apex and fall, dead. "Not for long. Hell, I'm only here to read from the lost preamble to the Codex of Zenghaus. I'm not here to kill anybody."

Just as they prepared to mount up one of the troopers shouted and pointed to the woods beside them where the men had emerged. A tall woman in a green gown peered from the thick brush.

Thynnes, clearly disgusted that his soldiers still wrestled with the intruders, spotted the woman and his face flushed. "Well, fuck me! Crown Princess Atirs!"

Nahum, a ginger haired trooper of some years on the job said what they all thought, "What is she doing down here away from the ceremony?"

Thynnes barked and Atirs jumped a little, "Fools, she probably ran from the attack up there. Yavin?"

From the men emerged an astonishing short soldier clad just like his fellows. Gorias guessed him barely five foot tall. As La

Beginning of the Trail

Gaul lamented that either his father was a big shot or there was no height restriction in the Transalpinan army, the youth stood at attention and barked back, "Sir!"

Thynnes ordered him, "Go look after her."

At these words, Atirs wore an expression of open-mouthed horror and fled into the woods.

Yavin hesitated but a curse on his mother from Thynnes made his boots work fast to pursue the Princess.

Gorias eyed Thynnes, who immediately shot back, "He doesn't fight like a bitch though."

"I didn't say anything."

"You think very loudly." Thynnes turned and shouted to the last trooper to arrive, "Jayred, fire a couple bolts over the summit of that hill! That'll stun them and buy us time."

Gorias guessed Jayred barely old enough to serve in the army much less shave, but the youth slid from his dancing pony and unslung a bow from his shoulder. He reached behind his head and slid an arrow from his quiver as Thynnes clashed swords with another priest. Involved in his own jab and parry move, Gorias missed Jayred notching the arrow. He then noted a glass ball on the tip of the missile with fluids sloshing inside it.

Thynnes right sword thrust extended too long and Gorias thought the priest would kill the old warrior, hell, he would've with such an opening even through the chain mail. Jayred drew his bowstring back as Thynnes let go of his blade and grabbed the hesitating priest by the wrist of his sword arm. The bolt flew from Jayred's touch as Thynnes pummeled the priest, punching him over and over in the face, his superior weight behind every shot. All of their action, even Thynnes' punches, ceased as the bolt exploded over the summit of the hill. The distant din of battle stopped as the mammoth burst of lights and rivulets of red color painted the air above the hill.

Thynnes let the priest go and his enemy fell to the ground. Once he reclaimed his sword, Thynnes skewered the priest in the chest as he walked away as casually as an old man plants a cane to bear himself up.

Gorias cleared out more of the priests, going low and hamstringing one with his left sword, but heard the bald man who didn't dismount with the troopers demand of the archer, "Kid, what's in that concoction?"

Jayred notched another arrow, laughed and replied, "Turak, I don't know, lots of chemicals, a bit of flame and a great deal of prayer."

The shortest of the robed figures reared back and lashed out at Jayred, unfurling the leather whip again. In a moment's time, the whip wrapped about Jayred's ankle as he stepped up to aim again, and tripped him. He stumbled and fell flat atop his missile, and it exploded under his body. Jayred's blood splattered Thynnes' boots and greaves.

Thynnes pointed at the shorter figure, whose hood came

back to reveal a girl probably no older than Jayred. "Well, curse the luck, there goes our archer. Get her, Cyrus and Nahum, dammit!"

Cyrus did step up to attack the whip girl, but Nahum stopped, staring at the body of Jayred. Gorias saw the young archer twitch as he died and the realization on Nahum's blank face of how fleeting life could be. The red-headed trooper had a harder look to him but Gorias guessed this the first time he'd smelt the guts of a friend.

Gorias confronted the one man who didn't dismount. "Turak? I'd never figure you to shy from a fight."

The bald man fished a flask from his waist belt, uncapped it and took a swig. "You all have it in hand. Looks like there'll be plenty'a killin' up the way, if they haven't sent the perfumed pricks to the bone orchard and fled."

Thynnes wore a disgusted look and mumbled, "Filthy mercenary." He then eyed Gorias. "But you're of royal blood way back. You are different." Thynnes let out a sarcastic laugh as he gave mocking applause to the troopers finally disarming the young woman using a whip. They had the girl by the shoulders and brought her to the General.

She spat on Thynnes' barreled chest and Gorias smirked, climbing back onto his horse.

Thynnes leered down at the girl and scratched his bearded chin. "You're no Pryten, but probably a pirate witch."

"I'm Noguria, daughter of..."

Thynnes grunted loudly, cutting her off as he went to his

horse. "You're just a girl in over your head."

Gorias' head swiveled around and he directed Traveler over to Noguria. He stabbed a finger at the jewel around her neck, and then leaned down low.

Cyrus' face flushed and he exclaimed, "It's an eye of the dragon! See the cut of the jewel?"

Before the others could close in, Gorias snatched the jewel in his hand and ripped the necklace off Noguria.

Thynnes got in the saddle, saying, "Your companions are dead and we don't have time for prisoners. I'd run if I were you."

Released, standing alone, Noguria licked her bottom lip, blood trickling from her teeth. She glared at Gorias as he prepared to go. She made an obscene gesture but Gorias ignored her.

Thynnes shouted, "The way you cut a swell with women is legendary indeed."

"The manners in young folks is gettin' terrible, maybe it'd be good if that story about the coming deluge is true, huh?"

"So much for you not killing anyone, aye?"

"Somebody always volunteers."

As they closed the short distance to the base of the hill, Turak pointed, shouting, "Look up there! Magicks!"

Gorias frowned. "Ya'd think a guy so covered in tattoos to bring healthy and easy wenches wouldn't be so scared of a few mages waving their pricks."

"Piss in your helm, La Gaul," Turak cussed him as they pulled up.

Gorias didn't debate the concept of fear of magic with a healthy respect. Any warrior worth their swords and had lived a few centuries had passed near enough to a mage to learn to stay out of their way. With the burst of green flame over the crest of the hill, Gorias hoped it was one of the Queen's wizards warding off their attackers.

An old saying came to Gorias as he watched two circular orbs tumble down the side of the hill: Heads will roll.

"Horse manure," Gorias muttered as he swung a leg over his black stallion Traveler and set his boots to the tall grasses. Two heads came to rest not far from his position. "Heads don't roll for shit."

"Ryss," Thynnes said, pointing at a figure in burgundy trousers and a doublet sporting frills on the sleeves. "He stands at the edge like he wants to run."

Gorias drew the twin blades from scabbards in the pack on his back. "Am I supposed to know who the fuck that is?"

Thynnes replied, "He's the consort of the Crown Princess back in the woods."

The troopers dismounted again and Turak started to climb down too, but a coughing fit stopped his motions. The two soldiers closest to Gorias stepped up and then quickly took a step back. Gorias disregarded it, as they were young.

Thynnes had no mercy on his men, nonetheless. "Don't fret

on the twin blades of Gorias La Gaul, you young pukes. If they are taken from angels wings or not doesn't mean squat."

"General Thynnes, yer all heart." Gorias threw back his washed out navy blue cloak and told the bald man off his horse at last. "Turak, we'll all be dead before you get your fat ass up the hill."

Turak drew a morning star from his saddle clasp and then a twin headed axe from across his saddlebags. "Good. A fool I was to ride along with you, La Gaul. This better be worth my trouble."

Gorias led them up the hill toward the din. "How was I to know the whores who serviced us also did this assassination squad for the royal family of Transalpina?"

Thynnes sucked air and started to lag behind Gorias. "The devils talk in their sleep to the sluts?"

Gorias boots dug in hard as they ran, "Why the young want to impress whores with their actions is beyond me."

A trooper made a joke about such men being politicians in training but Gorias couldn't match the voice to a face. He barely knew these young ones. Thynnes, he'd met decades ago when on a drunken lark to topple pervert King Silex of Albion. The fact that the General rode in the party Turak and he ran into on the way to this festival was pure chance. The young troopers wanted La Gaul with them and gushed to meet the legendary fighter from Thule.

Ryss walked back out of sight the closer they came to the top of the knoll. His casual gait didn't give the impression of worry. As they reached the crest of the hill that once supported the great stone circle many miles from the coast, Gorias thought that since he neared seven hundred years old, he'd not need to ever worry about acting the young fool again. Gorias loud war cry caused a brief pause to the action.

The flat top of the hill, about a half-acre in area, held a complex geometric pattern of polished logs and bodies, many still alive. Gorias ground his boot in the ring of gravel encircling the hilltop, denoting where the sacred ground began. He could see over the obstructions that the Queen stood in the center of the action, placid, hands folded in front of her teal gown. A flock of little girls surrounded Her Majesty and then a dwindling group of guards, using shields, swords and their bleeding bodies to stop an overwhelming force of men and women wearing the robes of priests. Gorias thought it a miracle Garnet still lived; perhaps the luck came from her wizards, who had seen better days by the look of them hugging the beams near to her, or the tenacity of her guards.

Gorias searched the carnage wrought by the flock of Pryten killers. Mildly, that idea amused him. The Prytens followed the ways of the Oak, and hated the Transalpinans for defiling their ancient stone circles and leveling their sacred groves. Gorias granted them that, not a belief in their system but anger at a superior civilization screwing them out of their land and sites. Garnet's grandfather had leveled this hill of the stone slabs, the remnants of which formed the gravel ring about this place. The sacred oak grove? Well, that's where the wooden beams came from that formed the sophisticated sphere of geometrically placed arches pleasing to the gods of Transalpina. Making an altar to a new god from the remains of an old god, Gorias mused, that reeked of bad business.

"They are but royalty, there are more of them in the world," Gorias shouted and threw off his cloak and donned his helmet. He swiped his swords across each other, releasing an ethereal spark. "Come get a taste of me, you pigs, and live forever."

The attackers of the royal party stepped back from their assault. They turned to face Gorias and a couple took pointed breaths. The sight of the towering man clad in blue dragon skin armor, wielding the lustrous short swords told them all his identity. Many whispered the name "La Gaul", the fable on two legs, the primordial warrior and whoremonger that left his bloody footprints across the world and spat in the face of the idea of the coming apocalypse by water.

The boast of Gorias divided the attackers, for truly a many wanted what he suggested, a place in the legend of Gorias La Gaul. They desired the spot at the end, the role of the one who slays him.

Two Prytens with clean-shaven faces charged him first, each holding a dagger in their left hand and a short handled single sided axe in the other. Gorias reckoned these clean cut two the better spies of the plot, as a Pryten savage couldn't get in close to royalty without being spotted.

"C'mon, you little punks," Gorias waited, putting his visor down, bouncing on the balls of his feet as they drew near, each planning to come at him from a side. "Deliverance will come."

As those with Gorias ran over the barrier and threw themselves into the great number of killers barely held at bay by the Queen's men, the two attacked Gorias. He dropped to his knees and they swung their axes, not surprised by his move, but over committed in their initial attacks. Gorias blades slashed down at diagonal lines, slicing cleanly through each of their shins. He worked his swords up, and ran the blades up between their legs, each weapon driving into a Pryten crotch. These cruel strikes landed hard and ended abruptly in each pelvic bone. They each smashed their axes on Gorias' body, the one on the left striking his shoulder, causing the axe head to bust off. The other struck Gorias' helm and knocked it off, but also broke his weapon.

Gorias stood, ripping his swords up further in each man, scraping off their bones and into their lower abdomens. His mound of ashen hair flowing out from the askew helmet, Gorias pulled the blades out and the Pryten on the left folded. The other wobbled, hands to his crotch before Gorias hooked a boot under the man's ankle and toppled him to the ground. He didn't bother giving them the deathblow to the heart. With their pricks ruined and loops of intestines spilling out into the sunshine, these men wouldn't be going anywhere soon.

General Thynnes and his troopers cut into the small army that attacked the royal party. Gorias saw that the Queen's guards, while skilled, had forfeited their lives for their monarch, save for a few that still stood. Many lay on the few stone benches left from antiquity not ground into gravel for the outer ring. These guards shook in their death rattles, streams of blood painting the grass once used for sacrifice to olden gods.

Turak made the hill at last and swung his morning star at a running naked Pryten. The spiked balls of Turak's weapon sank into the neck, chest and groin of a fleeing man. Turak yanked back, ripping the painted Pryten apart in three places. Turak didn't advance just yet but took time to brain the ruined man with his axe, too.

"Dumbass," Gorias spat. *Turak killed the man twice,* Gorias ruminated as he stepped further into the battle throwing a forearm smash into the face of a willing fighter. *No use for overkill on a day like today.*

One of the priests, a man much shorter than Gorias, leapt from behind a log configuration, but landed too close to him, swinging knives in each hand. Gorias couldn't hit him with his swords, so he dropped them, put up his arms and caught hold like a lover in a passionate embrace. Gorias ignored the knife blows to his armor and stomped his left boot onto the Pryten's sandaled foot. Although this shot hurt, it didn't cause nearly as much pain as when Gorias grappled him close again and yanked up, still stomping down with his boot, dislocating the ball joint of the Pryten's hip. Once he'd pushed off Gorias, the man fell, abandoning his knives to grab at his hip. Once Gorias snatched up his weapons, he flipped his swords about and drove them down like daggers into the Pryten's ribs.

On either side of the Queen, an emerald glow resonated around two figures clinging to wooden pillars. No, Gorias noted, not hugging--adhered or joined to the wood planks. Both wizards of the Queen bit it hard, victims of superior magicks, Gorias assumed they were clerics by the shiny robes to the god Seaxneat melted to the sizzling skin of two locked in an eternal embrace with the beams. Though two naked women covered in Pryten woad and tattoos lay deceased not far from each ruined wizard, two more stood not far away.

"Just as in any fight," Gorias said to Thynnes as he and the troopers surrounded the wizards. "They brought more guys, or girls." He then noted abnormally long snakes slithering around the bodies of these two dead mages. They rose up on their thin backs, supported by forked tails that wiggled but never rattled, searching with eyes very much like any man, not serpentine striped. That alone would give a common man the chills, but Gorias kept on.

The troopers looked at their leader, eyes full of terror. In moments, the Pryten shamans started to giggle, thin serpent's slithering about their necks and peering at the new arrivals. The soldiers started to shake violently.

Gorias felt the tinge of dark magick from these women, prickly on his whiskers like after a lightning strike. He and Thynnes exchanged a look before they struck fast with the swords in their right hands. Each man chopped a snake on the ground in half before they impaled a shaman, Thynnes striking through the guts, Gorias nailing the back, pushing his blade out the chest of his target. Thynnes worked his stab, twisting about in the body and shaking his own head around, saying, "Get outta my head, ya bitch!" fighting off the magicks of the shaman he struck. The General batted the head of the snake away with his armlet before it could strike him.

Gorias drew his blade out, but the lean snake encircled on his weapon, leaving its host to totter. He swished it in the air, vivisecting the serpent. Gorias then aimed with both swords at the wounded shaman, meaning to remove her head. Gorias blinked when his blades met at the neck bone and stopped. Perplexed, Gorias reckoned their magic strong enough to ward off his mystic blades that could pass through most anything alive. No one on the planet could channel their power much longer after a strike through the heart. Time showed him correct. Gorias felt the energy of that shaman, the very power of their god or demon, whatever gave them a point to focus their worship, pulled on his weapons. The invisible tug on his swords at the neck joints faded. Gorias heart fluttered but he dismissed it. His heart danced unruly more since he turned six hundred about a hundred years ago.

Beginning of the Trail

One of the Prytens stripped off his robe and leapt onto Gorias back, legs looping over the legend's thighs. The Pryten made the blunder most did in stabbing at Gorias' heart with a knife unable to penetrate dragon skin armor. Gorias knifed his swords into the ground and clenched the knees of his enemy. The assailant tried to gash Gorias' throat with the knife he broke on the dragon plating, but Gorias slanted his head. The serrated edge of the ruined blade connected with Gorias' bearded jaw, but scraped off on a jagged protruding bone hidden there. Gorias briefly thanked almighty God for a poorly healed busted jaw three centuries before and bit into the man's wrist. Still holding his enemy fast, Gorias fell backwards as if he plunged in a lake for a lark. Gorias full weight and armor crashed back to the ground, using the man on his back for a cushion. The Pryten's grappling hold released as the air left his body. Gorias wheeled over to his knees, and exposed the armlet of his armor, revealing the dew nail of the dragon there. The hooked nail passed across the Pryten's neck and only gore remained in its wake. Gorias stood again, taking up his swords, giving the dew nail and the Adam's apple stuck on there a mild look.

With most of the Pryten's dead or battling soldiers, Gorias shook off his armlet and joined Thynnes. Both stood looking into the final altar spot, both with blood in their beards, the pungent air very thick with gases from the dead. A lone man in good clothes stood not far from the Queen, not a speck of blood or dirt on him.

"Ryss," Thynnes whispered in a dismal voice, one not used on the noble families of the Queen.

All right, Gorias reasoned, *he's one of the royals left.* Ryss glared with rage at those who surrounded Queen Garnet, a gaggle of little girls in white silk tunics and lacey scarves. All of them had long faces, brown eyes and flowing hair, but ranged in ages from toddlers to pre-teens. Over a dozen girls formed a protective wall around the Queen, but her stern manner told him she didn't really hide behind them. If anything Garnet appeared as he remembered her: lots of starch in her panties, chin up, eyes clear, defiant, ready to accept his death surrounded by the maidens who attended her.

Ryss didn't let a few kids stop him. He turned about and lay hands on the Queen. That move on Garnet would've caused shock in public, but most folks who'd be enthusiastically aghast lay dead all around. The girls, however, didn't scream and scamper. No, they all attacked Ryss, each taking hold of a limb, a few at his midsection, all throwing punches and generally getting in the way.

Thynnes let his sword drop and gaped, along with everyone else on the hillside.

Gorias stepped forward as Ryss kicked a few of the girls away. Ryss wrestled them off his back fast. A couple of the kids hit the ground in front of Gorias, thus slowing his progress to get Ryss. One of the girls kicked off her sandal, put her thin hand through it, timed the shot and let Ryss turn his head toward her. She swung, connecting with Ryss' nose, breaking it austerely, causing blood to spray across the other girls. Baptized in blood, the kids fought on.

Beginning of the Trail

Angered, Ryss drew a knife from his tunic and swung at the tall teen, but she leaned back, avoiding the shot. Wading through little bodies, Ryss forgot the girl and staggered, grabbing at the Queen anew, first by the hem of her gown and then a handful of her thigh. Ryss held the Queen in a headlock, his left arm about her head, the curved dirk aimed toward her throat with his right hand.

Garnet never cried out, instead she punched Ryss in his already bloodied nose. Many might've figured her to slap him. Gorias didn't think that, however, for he knew she had great fortitude. All of her pluck and girls near her couldn't stop Ryss from pulling her near to hold a knife to her throat.

Thynnes swore, "Dammit, big hero, why didn't you get in there?"

Gorias could've asked him the same thing. He didn't believe Ryss would really slay her straight away, so he gambled, but didn't explain that to Thynnes. "I'm here to deliver the preamble of the great Codex to the Queen, and all of these dead Prytens are just gravy to the bill," Gorias spoke loud; making sure the man with desperate eyes heard him declare."of Gorias La Gaul."

The girls receded, all staring at the man holding their monarch, save for the girl who struck him in the nose. She studied Gorias, head tilted, quizzically.

Ryss snarled, "Back off, La Gaul."

Thynnes switched his sword to his left hand and held up his right. "Easy, Ryss."

Gorias walked in closer, but stopped a few yards from him. "There's nowhere to go."

"I'll kill her," he promised, jowls shaking a little, his taut face covered in a shield of sweat.

"Go ahead," Gorias told him with shrug as crows cried out overhead. "If ya do, only my word will tell the tale of what happens today. I'll get rich either way, but Garnet dead or no, get something straight, asshead…" Still gripping the pommel of his sword, Gorias pointed at him. "…*you* are gonna die."

"Big words. I hold the life of the Queen in my hands. An heir, the princess, will soon be in the arms of my Pryten allies. Things are going to change around this land, La Gaul, my Queen, Tancorix, will sit on the throne of Transalpina and you all will die, now back off!"

"I don't give a damn, I'm not from here." Gorias cleared his throat. "Now do it for the luvva God. I ain't gettin' any younger."

A puzzled look in his eyes, Ryss realized too late Gorias didn't speak to him. Gorias' eyes focused on the face of Garnet.

Ryss' body coiled as pain wound through his body, emanating from his groin. The queen stabbed her long nailed fingers into her holder's crotch and turned, making him move a few inches in his hold on her, enough for Garnet to drive her teeth into the hand holding the dirk. Amid the shouts and lurching moves of Ryss, Gorias charged, swords falling from his hands. His left grabbed the wrist of the hand Garnet still bit into. He squeezed and felt bones give way. Ryss' fingers opened and the grip on the dirk loosened. A swinging right fist connected with Ryss' left eye. Gorias wasn't sure if he broke the orbital bone there, but something pushed in under his touch. After he struck Ryss, he let his fist go flat and slapped over the top of the Queen's head. A firm grip on her locked in, Gorias took her scalp and moved her out of Ryss' arms.

Garnet flew back from the scene to the arms of General Thynnes. Gorias didn't release Ryss' wrist. "Done in by a woman," Gorias jeered him and gathered a handful of Ryss' velvet tunic, lifting his face up to meet a scorching stare. "Why the hell should you be any different?" Gorias kneed him in the groin and then swiped Ryss' trembling legs from under him, his hold still on the man's wrist. Ryss sprawled and Gorias held on, spiraling the arm and breaking the wrist at a crude angle. A few of the soldiers gasped as Gorias climbed on Ryss' back and secured a knee into the busted wrist. Ryss' screams muffled in the dirt as the big legend fixed him down.

"La Gaul," said Garnet as she tried to compose her breathing as she braced herself on the armored General protecting her. "Go easy, that's my kith and kin."

Gorias drove his knee into the busted wrist with more force and clenched a handful of Ryss' wavy hair. "Not any more he ain't." Ryss' face arose from the earth when Gorias yanked his head back, but took care not to fracture his neck. "Son in law, huh? I've heard of hating the mother in law, but this massacre takes the cake."

Garnet murmured, "We expected a plot..." She then cleared her throat and stood tall, her vitality returning, a regal method oozing from every pore. Even though in a blood stained full-length dress, Garnet stepped away from Thynnes a pace, hands together like mating spiders in front of her. "A scheme was in the air." Her voice, sturdy and prevailing, made one of the troopers take a knee. Another felt sheepish so he knelt, too.

Turak sucked wind over by a stone altar, pushed off a corpse and sat down, his hand wiping blood from his baldhead.

"From your own son in law? That is sweet," Gorias faced the man under his weight. "Ain't it?"

"We'll have your grand daughter," Ryss huffed. "The princess will be in the court of Tancorix in the Pryten wilderness within a day. The child will grow up with the savages and be a cannibal like all men should. You can kill me

"I will," Gorias promised as Thynnes beheaded one of the wizards stuck to the logs, ending his misery.

"...but the victory is only blunted," Ryss coughed and giggled. "All of your heirs will soon vanish and you will be a victim of the desires of Pergamus."

At the mention of the name, Gorias got off Ryss and turned him over. Hands on Ryss' chest, Gorias shouted, "What the hell did you say? Pergamus? Talk to me!"

"Burn in Hell, La Gaul."

"Hopefully not, but yer gonna see it before me." Gorias

got up and used Ryss' chest to stand on, making him wretch and squirm. Ryss couldn't escape under Gorias' boot. "Ma'am, where's your granddaughter?"

Her face unyielding, still as a statue speaking, Garnet answered, "At the royal home on the coast."

"The hunting lodge one where your papa used to breed horses?" Gorias could've added, *and many of the maids*, but he held his tongue.

"Yes. Do you think he tells the truth?"

"I'm gonna find out." He took his boot off Ryss, who quickly curled into the fetal position. "Hell, might be too late, but I'll get there as fast as Traveler can take me. It's not far."

"Gorias if they have her..."

He picked up his blades, wiping them off on Ryss' trousers before placing them back in the scabbards. "I'll get her back if I have to travel to the Pryten wilderness and kill ol' Tancorix herself."

Thynnes grunted before he added, "You'll need an army to do that."

"I might. We'll see. First things first."

Gorias reached to his side and pressed a series of snaps, opening a seam in his armor. He reached his hand inside with difficulty, grimacing to get at what he wanted. In a moment, Gorias withdrew out a shiny object all looked at in the daylight.

"That it? The damned preamble to the codex?" Thynnes asked, taking many breaths, his sword planted in the ground.

"The copper scroll of Hengest, the preamble to the great book of Zenghaus, lost for eons, kept by the Oracle of Wodan not far from Bospurus."

Garnet gave it scant attention. "No scroll, no magick makers could stop the hands of fate. Would that all wizards were burned and destroyed."

Gorias chuckled. "I thought maybe the Prytens came out after the scroll, as ya said it'd be here for the ceremony today."

The Queen rolled her eyes. "They wanted me dead. You over estimate your importance."

Thynnes interjected, "But I think they attacked before Gorias got here, figuring he'd be trouble if already there."

Garnet looked to the northwest like she could behold the Pryten wilderness. "War over the life of the princess?"

General Thynnes bowed his head to her and sucked in a breath. "Give that order, mum, and the army would be happy to root them out for you."

Garnet turned to Gorias. "What say you?"

"My words don't matter, I'm just a hired hand, leave me out of this local crap." He waved the scroll. "Sorry I showed up late. Reckon this doesn't matter any more."

"Not really."

Gorias shrugged and rolled up the scroll again. "Somebody will want it if you guys don't need it for the incantation and blessing."

Beginning of the Trail

"How many had to die for that scroll?"

"None, Ma'am," Gorias confessed, adjusting the snaps to his armor. "The Oracle of Wodan, Ivor, is an old friend. He handed it over to me as he felt it lacked importance."

Garnet's nose flared. "That was a flippant thing for this Oracle to do."

"He doesn't believe in your gods," said Gorias as the Queen turned away, looking at the last man still alive adhered to the wooden beams. He wagered her faith pretty slight about then, too. Gorias thought of putting the last wizard out of his misery, but noticed Cyrus and Nahum flipped a coin to decide who'd do it.

Ryss leapt up and reached out with his left hand for the scroll. He clasped the edge of it, but a chop from Gorias' left hand smashed Ryss back to the turf. The scroll fell to the ground while Gorias delivered an open handed slap across the face, buckling Ryss at the knees.

Thynnes picked up the scroll and squinted at the characters on the document.

Garnet watched him read and spoke in a strident voice, clear enough for the survivors and soldiers to hear. "There was nothing clandestine in Lord La Gaul's appearance. Many were aware that he would bring the fabled preamble to the Codex for the ceremony for Eostre. The event would heighten in its importance, which is why so many of the royals came out just to see him." She stared at Thynnes who still read. "Men would kill for what you hold, General, and pay dearly to have it. Imagine, an impossibly rare document like that in the possession of a monarch, exclusive to what it says, a dearly revelatory experience for the one who keeps it."

Facing the sky, his right hand shielding his eyes from the sun, Gorias commented, "The holder of that could dispel a great many myths about various faiths and start a new form of devotion if they so chose."

"Yes," Thynnes nodded. "I think that'd be so."

Gorias cracked his knuckles, eyes shut, recalling exactly what the scroll said: *"Dear Gorias La Gaul. A great scheme to assassinate the royal family of Transalpina is underway. I cannot tell who the usurpers are, but I have a wicked suspicion my son-in-law, Ryss, is among them. I've not trusted him since the death of my daughter's first husband on the hunt in Albion. Please attend the festival of Lammas and get them into the open. We shall say you're bringing me the fabled lost preamble to the Codex of Zenghaus. They will fear the revelations therein and strike. They are surely controlled by religious fanatics across the channel. If not, they'll be the first agnostics to want to seize a throne. I have my loyal guards, but any plotters will be after you and the idea of a consecrated scroll. They have a stratagem, my ears on the wall say, but I cannot tell when it will be executed. Hopefully, this will force their hand. If I am wrong, then we will have to figure another strategy. You will be well compensated. G.P."*

Thynnes cleared his throat and rubbed his fingers together,

feeling Gorias' blood that had tainted the scroll. "Thanks for bringing this, Gorias." He handed it to the Queen. "You better keep that, Mum. I wouldn't feel right about holding it."

Eyes on the General, Gorias wondered, "So, what do ya think, Thynnes? That sound like the word a'God to you?"

Scratching his cheek above where his beard terminated, Thynnes fell silent for a few moments. "Yeah. Not everyone needs to know such things."

"What's with all of the little girls?" Gorias asked Thynnes, gesturing with his right hand at the girls meandering around but shadowing the Queen, changing the subject.

Turak sucked on his flask, leaned back on the altar and said, "They must belong to the dead aristocrats here for the ceremony. Sure a lot of them came out for the ceremony of dedication. Probably bloodier than they counted on, huh?"

Thynnes shot him a poisonous look then faced Gorias. "You keep bizarre company."

"Just another hired hand met on the road, he isn't my brother."

Garnet rolled up the scroll and slid it into her sleeve as Gorias rubbed at a few of the splotches of blood on his face, smudging them worse, but accenting his weathered face in the sunlight.

Thynnes informed him, "These are the daughters of General Appra. I think he has twenty of them and no sons."

"Huh. Where's the General? I haven't seen in him in decades."

"He's not a palace sentinel, but the ol' boy is dying."

"A shame, but his daughters stuck by their Queen, bless 'em." He watched as Nahum and other soldiers took count of the dead citizens, who came for a religious ceremony and to kiss the Queen's ass, but ended up worm food. "Too bad the aristocracy ate it so hard, but they fought well in death."

Thynnes frowned. "On the bright side, they cleared out a buttload of snobs."

The Queen turned fast to face her General. "Many were members of the royalty family, however distant. Where is my daughter? Is she among the dead? I cannot even tell you who my only heir is now. Perhaps Princess Nykia is the last one left."

Cyrus stepped up, saluted, and announced, "She was at the bottom of the hill with the guys that tried to stop us, sir. Remember?"

Thynnes' look didn't improve. "Yes, soldier, I recall."

Cyrus pulled his baldric off, bowed to the Queen and then stepped close to Gorias. He opened his mouth but didn't speak.

"What?"

"Is it true your swords came from an angel's wings?"

Gorias glared at the Cyrus and exhaled noisily. "Is it true your daddy wanted a son?"

He turned and heard Thynnes admonish the soldier. "Don't ask Lord La Gaul about that nonsense or dragons, you damned idiot!"

Meekly, the soldier replied, "Because he killed so many?"

Thynnes replied, "Because he killed the last one."

The tallest of the girls knelt by the dead snakes, her brown eyes soon caught Gorias' gaze. She asked him, "aren't snakes blind?"

"That's the idea, I think," he replied and turned from Ryss.

"Why are the eyes blue and like a person?"

Gorias squatted to his haunches as he checked the bodies close to her. "Valid question. I don't think they are snakes proper, like something in the jungle or even the striped bull snakes around these parts." He pointed to the body of the Pryten shaman that fell face up. "See the marks on her teats?"

Garnet admonished him. "La Gaul, Alena's a baby girl."

Alena's eyes filled with curiosity where Gorias indicated. "There are holes by her tips."

"Yeah on her nipples," Gorias said and winked at Garnet, who grimaced and faced away from them. "That shaman has marked between her boobs, too. This thing here fed off her, probably her soul too. Witches have an extra teat on them to suckle the Devil, that's an old wives tale, but the port is to really feed blood directly to their creations."

Alena blinked and stood, her bare foot nudging the split tail of one of the dead snakes. "Look at the ends of those double tails. They have five little bumps like toes."

"Ya got better eyes than me, missy," Gorias declared. "If

they're growing feet and had eyes like people, glad I killed them."
He ruffled her hair. "I'll tell that to the next old wife I see."

Alena took the lacy scarf from her head and doubled it over
in her hand. She applied it to Gorias' blood soaked beard on the
right side.

Gorias put his hand on hers and his blood ran through his
brushy beard and wetted both of their hands. "Thanks."

"Does it hurt?" Alena quizzed him and patted his wet beard.

Gorias winked. "Kinda. Ya get used to pain."

Alena bit her bottom lip and then stared at her scarlet colored
fingers. "Will you be all right?"

"Probably not, but I ain't lucky enough to die easy." Gorias
reached down and took Ryss' broken wrist. "Yer comin' along for
the ride, son-in-law."

Not caring how much Ryss screamed, Gorias dragged him to
the bottom of the hill, he threw him down by Traveler and started
to dig in his saddlebags.

The short soldier Yavin emerged from a wooded area nearby
carrying a body nearly twice his size.

The Queen, helped down the hill by Alena, hurried over to
Yavin. "Atirs, my daughter, the mother of the princess."

Yavin showed no fatigue for his burden. "I thought she fled in
terror, but she drew a knife and tried to kill me. I let her run, what
could I do, mum?"

Tongue out of her mouth, Atirs' chest lay still. Gorias saluted the small soldier not just for his strength in his task, but the guts to present a corpse to the Queen and not piss himself.

No tears in her eyes or voice, the Queen asked, "What happened?"

"She drank something." A small ceramic vial fell from Yavin's grip from under Atirs' back. He lay her down on the long grasses. "She's gone." Yavin bowed his head, snatched up the vial and offered it to Thynnes.

The General sniffed it. "I'm no judge of poisons. We should ask the herbalist Yannick on that one."

From behind them, a respectful distance, Nahum sang out, "Isn't Yannick dying of the blood sickness coming out his backside?"

Thynnes cursed, "Who isn't fucking dying these days?"

Gorias pulled a circle of rope from his saddlebags, let it plunge to the ground and walked past the Queen. He took the body of the Queen's daughter and laid it not far from her sobbing husband. Gorias then flipped Atirs over and ripped her dress open. Again, the crowd held their breath at his actions.

"You guys are too damned sensitive," Gorias muttered and pointed, the bloody scarf in his hand. "See? Those are tiny tattoos."

The flustered Queen struggled not to sob. "What? So what?"

"They are Pryten marks." From his haunches, Gorias looked up and told her. "Your daughter had pledged her loyalty to Tancorix, ma'am. Those marks are devoted to their goddess, Hretha."

"The bitch," Garnet growled and turned away.

Gorias wasn't sure who she spoke of, the goddess, Tancorix or her own daughter. He still had a job to do. Gorias stepped over and backhanded Ryss in the face. "Hey, piss ant."

"Wha?" he started, stunned by the fresh shot. "What are you doing to me?"

"Taking you to see your daughter." Gorias told him as he ran the rope under Ryss' arms, between his legs, then all around his body. He then tied it to his saddle. Gorias soon produced another rope and spun it about the body of the Queen's daughter. Gorias strapped her to the wailing man. "Here, I got company for ya. It'll be a rough ride."

Garnet stood near the two lashed together, holding hands with Alena. "It's all my fault, Gorias. I should've not weakened when her first husband died out on the hunt. This one, barely known in the land, appeared as a ready tissue for her tears. I felt that pang of objection, but as I'm getting on, I hated to deny her happiness."

"What were the odds he was an agent of Tancorix?"

"Who could've thought it?"

"Don't just blame yourself. Your wizards are shitty judges of character or in league with them. Ya tell me they didn't have a clue or inkling in the ether realm that something was amiss? Killing all them pricks sounds like a great start to a peaceful kingdom."

Garnet thought for a moment. "Perhaps I could torture the wizards and see."

Beginning of the Trail

"Good idea, beats buying them muffins," Gorias said under his breath. "I better hit it fast."

Thynnes said, "We'll go along."

Gorias snapped, "No, I'll do just fine alone. There just might be an insurrection going on in this land. You stay and guard the Queen. Ya never know if a fresh bunch of assassins or a group of booger-men wait in those woods for Garnet's head. Get her and the rest back to Qesot. They will be safer in the capitol city."

Turak coughed, took another quaff from his flask and lamented, "Wonder why Garnet and this land is so important? Albion is closer to the Pryten wilderness and a pretty nice place."

Eyes on the bloody cloth in his hand, Gorias said quietly, "Pergamus."

Hands balled to fists, Thynnes barked at Gorias, "Who? What's Pergamus?"

"Some say it's a place, others a person, the land where Satan dwells, the island where a fallen angel plots ways to never go to the abyss and avoid the coming deluge."

Garnet sighed. "Do you really think all of that talk of a deluge is true? Rollers of bones have said the world will end for ages. Why do so many accept this fate by water one hears on the winds?"

"Maybe if even the demons are scared of it there's a hint of truth to it."

"Why do you speak of Pergamus?"

"Because assface Ryss here knows something, but won't tell.

No way to get it out of him so, thems the breaks."

Gorias donned his helmet and climbed into the saddle. Traveler careened about and Gorias saluted the queen. "I'll bring back your princess, ma'am."

The Queen studied the two lashed together. Gorias half expected her to wring her hands, but that wouldn't be Garnet. She had nothing to be guilty for. She'd not allow such an emotion in her being.

"Am I so unjust that they want me dead?"

"Naw," Gorias shrugged and stretched his back. "I doubt it is personal, you're just in the way of plans too big for this world."

She raised her eyes to Gorias. "You're close to seven hundred now, aren't you?"

"Heh, who is counting, ma'am?"

"I'm over a hundred now. Does everyone where you hail from live so long?"

"I think this world is full'a people that need to die, um, natural like. Hell, I dunno, ma'am. If I had all the answers, they'd be buildin' a shrine to me."

Thynnes smirked. "They'd serve beer at yours, Gorias, not wine there."

Hands tight on his reins, Gorias asked her, "How did you come to suspect your daughter?"

"Aside from her acting distant, I heard her cry out to Hretha when she climaxed."

Beginning of the Trail

At the name of the Pryten goddess, Thynnes slapped his hand to his forehead and Gorias shook his head. There was no mandate on belief in Transalpina, Gorias reflected as he studied the sky for a moment. One could believe in any god one chose, save for the Pryten ones. Somewhere in the mists of time's dawn these two cultures decided they hated each other, down to their gods. Transalpina advanced in civilization and technology while the Pryten lands were full of tribal fights and regressed. Queen Tancorix over there was as close to a uniting figure the Pryten's possessed even in Gorias' living memory.

Garnet welled with tears for a moment, but fought it down with all the grace of a man breaking a horse. He admired her guts, but also understood such shedding of emotion could eat a hole in one's soul.

Thynnes drew close to Gorias. "What if the attack on the hill never happened? What if you showed up and were expected to give a revelation from that phony scroll?"

"Pubic speaking is mostly bullshit and experience. If I'd have rode up to a peaceful setting, you'd have got to experience my bullshit."

Once more, Garnet eyed the two at her feet. "Is this necessary?"

"Yeah," Gorias replied, waved a hand at the troopers and little girls watching from the top of the hill. "Actions speak loud, they say, but words carry the acts to all." He held up the bloody cloth and said to Alena, "I'm keeping this, young lady."

Alena grinned and curtseyed to him.

Gorias kicked his heels in Traveler and they bolted away, dragging the screaming Ryss tied to his dead wife behind him.

Gorias figured the Queen comprehended the lesson, that every one of those sons of bitches on the hill would tell everyone they knew what they saw him do that day. The message was unambiguous: This is the fate of those who harm the Queen. Aside from her guards, something even worse guarded Queen Garnet's interests. Gorias had known the Queen since she was a lass and understood her love of being respected, and feared.

Traveler galloped hard and only half the intent became realized. Gorias laughed that this part would make the story even better.

After an hour on the trail, Gorias met a huge company of cavalry wearing the colors of Transalpina. At the sight of him they spread out, but never drew their weapons. A single rider came forward to greet Gorias, who didn't draw his twin blades. The rider stopped short as the troopers all whispered "La Gaul" with one voice.

Gorias called out, "Let me pass, son, I have shit to do."

The soldier pulled his face wrap to one side and nodded. "We heard tell you were in country, Lord La Gaul."

"I ain't a Lord no more."

"I'm Captain Harlan."

Beginning of the Trail

"Good for you." Gorias kept his stern way up for them, but his fatigued body felt grateful for the quick respite.

Harlan faced the two bodies bound up behind Gorias mount, mangled by the abuse of the countryside. He glanced at his men who focused on the bodies. With a desiccated voice, Harlan told him, "There are forces of revolt all over. The army and navy are meeting it fast."

"Great, now I gotta go save the princess."

"We are on our way to the capitol."

"Ya want a cookie? I gotta light a shuck for the coast."

Harlan blinked, mouth wide, but looked down at the tied up bodies as Ryss cried out, "Help me! We are of the royal house of Lady Garnet! This man has killed the crown princess and is torturing me!"

The cavalrymen gawked at each other as Harlan demanded, "What did he say?"

"Never mind him, he's fuckin' drunk." With that, Gorias kicked Traveler and set off again for the coast. None of the men on horseback followed.

Several miles before he reached the coastal lodge of the Queen's family, her daughter fell off someplace. Wild dogs, rats or monsters in the night would feed on the corpse for all he knew and that was all right.

Gorias rode hard, but that didn't stop him from reaching into one of the pouches on his belt and pulling out Noguria's jewel. He eyed it in the sunlight as he rode, nodded and then braced his left arm on the saddle horn. From the plates of armor on his forearm protruded the dragon's dew nail. Reins to his teeth, Gorias took the jewel and rubbed it on the point of the dragon nail. A few strokes later, the jewel burst and turned to countless shards, blowing away in the winds as he went on.

Eyes closed for a moment, Gorias felt another tremor from his chest and the name Pergamus returned to him. He hadn't pondered Pergamus for a century. Many thought Pergamus a mysterious island where pirates talked to a spirit oracle, but Gorias knew better. Pergamus wasn't a place. It was a he. A fallen angel, the father of all dragons who mated with saurian beasts instead of women like his cursed brothers. They created giants, Nephilums and such. What Pergamus might want in Transalpina via Tancorix intrigued him. Gorias didn't want to die finding out, but it interested him all the same. Only a clairvoyant could sort it all out, he thought.

Clouds overhead cast baggy silhouettes over the rolling green valleys. The territory grew steeper as the air blew cooler from the nearing ocean. Gorias stopped to rest a few times, quickly chewing on old jerky and a stale biscuit in his bag. Once he washed that down with water from his canteen, he glanced back at Ryss who moved a little still. Still tired and hungry, Gorias put all of that out of his mind for his task had only just started.

He smiled in spite of himself at the ruse of the codex. There was no such thing. The preamble of that Codex didn't exist and never had, save for on the tongues of those who made legends. Gorias pondered that he rode the pages of created fables like an expert equestrian. How many words passed in taverns or palace mead halls made him more potent, powerful and stronger than he really was?

Gorias didn't know when Ryss expired precisely, but he still dragged him to the seaside lodge. By the time he hit the beach where the Pryten's had their rafts moored, the body of the traitor lay nearly flailed of its skin, unrecognizable.

Down the beach the miscreant Prytens carried the little dark haired princess, but she didn't scream. They wrestled her toward one of boats as waves lapped the sand, haphazard and foaming. A woman in a robe, painted up with woad, probably a shaman, spotted him riding on the beach.

He drew his blades, put his reins in his teeth and charged, thinking, perhaps overkill would be the course of the day.

To be continued...

About the Author

Steven L. Shrewsbury, from Central Illinois, enjoys football, history, politics and good fiction. Over 300 of his short stories have been published in print or digital media. His small press novels include OVERKILL, HELL BILLY, THRALL, BAD MAGICK, BEDLAM UNLEASHED, STRONGER THAN DEATH, HAWG, TORMENTOR, GODFORSAKEN, the forthcoming PHILISTINE and BLACK SON RISING. These titles run from horror to historical high fantasy. He tries to drown out the rumors that he is Robert E. Howard reincarnated with beer. When not wrangling his sons, he can be found outside in his happy place.

Transcend reality with Seventh Star Press!

On the following pages we would like to introduce you to some of our titles featuring Sword and Sorcery, Post-Apocalyptic Fantasy, Epic Fantasy, YA Fantasy, and more!

To get more information on Seventh Star Press and our titles, please visit:

www.seventhstarpress.com

or connect with us at:
www.twitter.com/7thstarpress
www.facebook.com/seventhstarpress

More Gorias adventures from Steven Shrewsbury!
Enter an ancient world of heroes, blood, and steel in the
tales of Gorias La Gaul! Hard-hitting Sword & Sorcery in
the vein of Robert E. Howard!.

Softcover ISBN: 9781937929800

eBook ISBN: 9781937929831

Softcover ISBN: 9780983108634

eBook ISBN: 9780983108641

Grand Epic Fantasy from Stephen Zimmer!
Explore the world of Ave in the Fires in Eden Series from
Stephen Zimmer! Epic Fantasy for those who enjoy authors
like George R.R. Martin and Steven Erikson!

Softcover ISBN: 9780982565612

eBook ISBN: 9780982565698

Softcover ISBN: 9780983108627   Softcover ISBN 9781937929855

eBook ISBN: 9780983108610   eBook ISBN 9781937929862

Explore post-apocalyptic fantasy worlds in the Seventh Star Press anthology *The End Was Not the End*, from editor Joshua H. Leet!

softcover ISBN: 978-1-937929-07-7
eBook ISBN: 978-1-937929-15-2

Action-driven Fantasy from D.A. Adams!
Begin your journey into The Brotherhood of Dwarves, the
popular YA Fantasy series from D.A. Adams. An action-
filled saga where the dwarves are not just sidekicks!

Softcover ISBN: 9781937929916   Softcover ISBN: 9781937929923

eBook ISBN: 9781937929930   eBook ISBN: 9781937929-947

Softcover ISBN: 9780983740254   Softcover ISBN: 9781937929787

eBook ISBN: 9781937929909   eBook ISBN: 9781937929770

YA Fantasy From Jackie Gamber!
The highly-acclaimed Leland Dragon Series from Jackie
Gamber! Strong character-driven YA Fantasy for those
who enjoy authors such as Christopher Paolini.

Softcover ISBN: 9780983108672

eBook ISBN: 9780983108696

Softcover ISBN: 9781937929893

eBook ISBN: 9781937929817

Be sure to check out the other novella-sized single-author collections of short stories from Seventh Star Press!

Also available!

Have many action-driven fantasy adventures in the world of Ave in Stephen Zimmer's *Chronicles of Ave, Volume 1*.

Softcover: 978-1-937929-30-5
eBook: 978-1-937929-31-2

Want more Sword and Sorcery?
Pick up the anthologies *Thunder on the Battlefield:*
Sword, and *Thunder on the Battlefield: Sorcery,*
from editor James R. Tuck!
(author of the Deacon Chalk novels)
Available in print and eBook!

Thunder on the Battlefield: Sword
Softcover: 978-1-937929-24-4
eBook: 978-1-937929-25-1

Thunder on the Battlefield: Sorcery
Softcover: 978-1-937929-26-8
eBook: 978-1-937929-27-5